✔ KU-531-032

MEANT-TO-BE MUM

BY
KAREN TEMPLETON

MILLS & BOON

All rights reserved including the right of reproduction in whole or in part in any form. This edition is published by arrangement with Harlequin Books S.A.

This is a work of fiction. Names, characters, places, locations and incidents are purely fictional and bear no relationship to any real life individuals, living or dead, or to any actual places, business establishments, locations, events or incidents. Any resemblance is entirely coincidental.

This book is sold subject to the condition that it shall not, by way of trade or otherwise, be lent, resold, hired out or otherwise circulated without the prior consent of the publisher in any form of binding or cover other than that in which it is published and without a similar condition including this condition being imposed on the subsequent purchaser.

® and ™ are trademarks owned and used by the trademark owner and/or its licensee. Trademarks marked with ® are registered with the United Kingdom Patent Office and/or the Office for Harmonisation in the Internal Market and in other countries.

Published in Great Britain 2015
by Mills & Boon, an imprint of Harlequin (UK) Limited,
Eton House, 18-24 Paradise Road, Richmond, Surrey, TW9 1SR

© 2015 Karen Templeton-Berger

ISBN: 978-0-263-25128-9

23-0415

Harlequin (UK) Limited's policy is to use papers that are natural, renewable and recyclable products and made from wood grown in sustainable forests. The logging and manufacturing processes conform to the legal environmental regulations of the country of origin.

Printed and bound in Spain
by CPI, Barcelona

Karen Templeton is a recent inductee into the Romance Writers of America Hall of Fame. A three-time RITA® Award-winning author, she has written more than thirty novels for Mills & Boon and lives in New Mexico with two hideously spoiled cats, has raised five sons and lived to tell the tale, and could not live without dark chocolate, mascara and Netflix.

MORAY COUNCIL LIBRARIES & INFO.SERVICES

20 38 96 75	
Askews & Holts	
RF	

This book is dedicated to everyone who's ever doubted their ability to fix something. Especially when it looked hopeless. But they did it anyway. Because they were too stubborn to give up, or listen to the naysayers. You are my people.

Chapter One

"**D**ad. Dad!"

His brain already in knots from grocery shopping with a pair of adolescents, Cole Rayburn frowned at his shivering twelve-year-old daughter. Who was clearly about to freeze in her tank top and short-alls in the frigid store, despite the curtain of blond hair shielding her bare shoulders. But would she listen to Cole's suggestion to take a sweater with her? Oh, hell, no—

The slight note of alarm in Brooke's voice belatedly registered, echoing through his entire nervous system. Not that he'd let her see it—

"What is it, honey?"

"That man over there," she whispered, sidling closer to Cole's elbow. Much as she'd done for the past week, as if afraid he'd disappear if she let him out of her sight. Gratifying and terrifying all at once. "No, the one by the apples. With the white hair. He keeps staring. Like he knows us or something." A few feet away, her slouching, dark-haired brother, Wesley, gawked at a towering display of canned soda. Longingly. Cole briefly met his son's silent plea, ignored both the stab of guilt and Wes's sigh, then finally looked to see who Brooke was talking about.

And damned if his own adolescence didn't flash before his eyes.

He'd assumed, of course, he'd eventually run into one or more of the family he'd practically grown up with. Just not this soon. Or that he'd have such mixed feelings about the reunion, even after all this time.

Or whether the man everyone called the Colonel would be more inclined to welcome him home like the Prodigal Son…or splatter his guts all over the grapefruit.

"Cole?" Preston said. Grinning, actually. So far, so good. "Cole Rayburn?"

"Yes, sir," Cole said, returning the grin, even as he reminded himself it'd been more than twenty years since Sabrina Noble had dragged home, like a stray puppy, the flabby dork he used to be. The Colonel still had a couple of inches on him—although, at six-four, he pretty much towered over everybody—but Cole understood why the older man hadn't recognized him at first. Few people from those days would.

By now they were side by side, their carts facing opposite directions like a pair of horse riders meeting up on a trail. Unlike Cole, the Noble clan patriarch hadn't changed a whole lot that Cole could tell. Although he had to be in his seventies by now, the retired air force officer had lost none of the imposing bearing that had gone a long way toward keeping his motley group of adopted and foster children in line for so many years. The shoulders were still square, the posture still ramrod straight, his intense blue gaze as direct as ever. But not, Cole could see now that he was closer, as bright.

It also occurred to him he couldn't remember Preston

ever doing the grocery shopping. That had been his wife Jeanne's domain.

Now he clasped Cole's hand in a firm shake. All forgiven? Forgotten? Unknown? Although Sabrina would've had to say something, wouldn't she? To explain—

"Didn't mean to creep you out," the Colonel said, "but I wasn't sure it was you at first. What on earth are you doing back here, boy? Thought you'd fled New Jersey years ago."

Cole smiled. "I'm only in Maple River for the summer. Taking care of my parents' place while they're away." He grinned down at Brooke, frowning so hard Cole had to fight a laugh. "This is my daughter, Brooke. And this guy," he said as Wes wandered back, curiosity clearly overriding— for the moment—his annoyance with his father's junk-food ban, "is my son, Wesley. Kids, this is Preston Noble. Spent a lot of time at his house, when I was around your age."

Because I had the mother of all crushes on your daughter, sir.

And how is Sabrina, by the way?

The Colonel's brows dipped slightly behind his glasses, as if he knew exactly what Cole was thinking. Which wouldn't surprise him in the least. It used to rattle all the kids, Preston's uncanny ability to read their minds, to put the kibosh on trouble before they could get into it. Most of the time, anyway.

But not all.

Both kids politely shook the older man's hand, although Brooke hung back, more like a much younger child would have. Not surprising, Cole supposed, considering recent events.

And damned if the Colonel didn't somehow pick up on that, too, immediately engaging both kids in some tale or other from when Cole had been a fixture in the Nobles' kitchen, when Jeanne Noble had known his food preferences better than his own mother. And as he watched his still shell-shocked children begin to thaw in the warmth of the older man's spirited tale-telling, he realized he couldn't ever remember the Colonel talking down to a kid, how he always treated them as the intelligent, capable beings he knew, and expected, them to be. Not surprisingly, the kids were eating it up. Same as Cole had.

Then the older man met Cole's gaze, his smile almost wistful. "The three of you should come over. So we can catch up properly. Not in the middle of the Food Lion."

"Oh. Um...I..."

"How about this afternoon? If you're not busy, I mean. Jeanne's roses are spectacular this year, with all this rain. She would've been so pleased. You remember, I'm sure, how much she loved those roses."

Loved. Past tense.

Cole's heart lurched in his chest. That explained the slightly not-there look in the older man's eyes. Why *he* was shopping.

"I'm sorry. I didn't know."

"No reason you should have. Eight years ago now."

"But you still have the house?"

"For now. Since everyone's out on their own..." Preston's attention drifted back to the kids, now quietly arguing over grapes. Or something. "The boy looks exactly like you, doesn't he?"

"Except about fifty pounds lighter."

The older man turned back to him. "You'd already lost a lot of it, though, by your junior year." He chuckled. "When you shot up six inches in as many months. Jeannie said you never saw it. Your metamorphosis."

Cole felt his face warm. "I...no. I guess I didn't."

The Colonel humphed, clearly keeping whatever else he was thinking to himself as he looked back at the bickering duo. "It's not like I don't see the others fairly often, since they're all still around. Well, except for Sabrina, she's in New York. Pretty much only comes back for weddings. And new babies. And we've got plenty of those. Still.

It's not like it used to be, when the house was filled." He paused. "Too damn big now," he said softly. "Too quiet."

The longing in the older man's voice knifed straight through Cole, partly because he doubted Preston even realized it was there. If it was one thing the guy wasn't, it was manipulative. Anal and demanding, perhaps, he thought with a smile, but definitely not one to play the pity card. And since his own parents were away—and had never been the coddling grandparent types, anyway—and Erin's parents were both dead, what could it hurt to the let the old guy play honorary grandpa for an hour or so?

And frankly, Cole wouldn't mind seeing the house again. If for no other reason than to perhaps expunge a memory or two.

"We're having dinner with my sister tonight," he said, "but I suppose we could come over for a little while this afternoon."

Preston beamed. "That would be great. Around two or so?"

"We'll be there."

The other man clapped him on the shoulder before steering his cart down the aisle. Cole watched him for a second, then wandered over to the veggie section, ignoring his children's grimaces as he bagged a bunch of broccoli and plunked it into the cart. "Heads up—we're going to go visit Colonel Noble later."

"Why?" Wesley said, suspicious.

"Because he invited us. And it'll be fun, getting to see the house again."

Fun. Yeah. Let's go with that.

"One of his kids…" To Cole's surprise, his throat caught. He cleared it, then said, "Was my best friend, all through middle and high school."

"What was his name?"

He tossed a three pack of multicolored peppers into the

cart. "*Her* name." And some asparagus, tightly rubber-banded. "Sabrina."

"Your best friend was a girl."

"Yep."

Wesley shook his head as Brooke leaned on the front of the cart, impeding Cole's progress. "How come you never mentioned her before?"

"I'm sure I did. I must have."

"Nope. I would've remembered. So how come?"

Did he dare try Brussels sprouts on them? He did.

"Haven't seen her in years. One of those things."

And amazingly he sounded almost nonchalant. In the past, over and done, didn't matter. Highly doubtful he'd ever see her again.

Except Brooke gave him one of her strange looks, her searing, green-eyed stare reminding him yet again that he was perpetually an inch away from screwing up. Especially now. But at least, for these few minutes, he'd managed to distract them from what must have been the constant refrain of their mother's pulling the rug out from under them. Completely of their own volition and without Cole's knowledge, his extraordinarily courageous children had given his ex the choice between them and a lifestyle that had left them feeling like also-rans—and she had not chosen them.

And this—they—did matter. *Now* mattered. In a way that nothing else ever had, or ever would. Because while his love life was apparently doomed to eternal suckage, these kids would know they came first. That he loved them, and was proud of them, and wanted nothing less than the best for them.

Even if that included tiny cabbage-like vegetables, so innocently snuggled together in their little green net, unaware of their own gross-out factor. Awesome. "Dinner. Tomorrow," he said. Both kids groaned, and Cole smiled.

Maybe he had no idea what he was doing, but at least they'd know he cared.

* * *

Blowing out a breath, Sabrina Noble stuffed her wallet back inside her purse as the taxi chugged away behind her down the tree-lined street. Shadow and sunlight danced across the lawn like a thousand fairies, beckoning her up the wide, welcoming stairs fronting the serene Queen Anne.

Home.

As in, that place you go when your future gets shot out from under you. Although not for long, the for-sale sign reminded her. She frowned, still not entirely sure how she felt about that.

A rose-scented breeze—not a smell one often caught in Manhattan, if ever—tangled with her long hair, and made her shiver slightly underneath her floaty top. Although not because she was cold.

Squaring her shoulders, Sabrina trudged up the brick walk, her largest rolling bag *clackety-clacking* behind her, echoing the refrain in her head—that she had no intention of staying a minute longer than necessary. She lugged the bag up onto the porch, returning to the curb for the rest of her luggage before retrieving the spare key from the secret pocket on the underside of the striped cushion on the far rocker. The front door open, she breathed in that same faint scent of eucalyptus she'd always associate with her childhood. With her adoptive mother, Jeanne, who'd installed that "secret" pocket. Amazing, that they'd never been robbed.

Although they had been, actually, of the woman who'd *loved* more than any human being Sabrina had ever known.

The sting of tears startled her. Never mind she'd lived on her own since she graduated from college. But if Mom had been here, there would have been hugs and cookies and sympathy. And probably a good talking-to, about needing to buck up and move on. And then more hugs—

Blowing out a breath, Sabrina hauled the bags inside

and shut the door…only to frown when, from the back of the house, came a girl's high-pitched giggle, followed by another kid's—a boy?—affronted response. Then a masculine rumble, definitely not Pop's, gently rebuking. For a second, irritation spiked, that Pop wasn't alone. And wasn't that stupid? That she was annoyed, not that he had company. Giving her head a sharp shake, she shoved down the case's handle, let her purse slither off her shoulder to softly thunk onto the worn entryway carpet—

Like a summoned genie, the man she and her twin brother, Matt, had called their father since they were kindergartners appeared in the foyer. Underneath bristly white hair, ice-blue eyes slammed into hers.

"Sabrina? What are you doing here? The wedding's not for another week—"

"Surprise," she said through a tight throat, and her father's eyes narrowed. Between two decades in the military and a second "career" fostering more kids than Sabrina could count, nothing got past Pop. Especially a small mountain of luggage sprawled across his foyer rug.

His gaze veered back to hers, burgeoning with questions.

"Later," she whispered. More laughter drifted out from the kitchen. "When we're alone—"

"Preston?" she heard, a split second before the dude belonging to the deep voice materialized behind him. And if it hadn't been for the steely gray eyes, that one stubborn, still untamed curl at his temple, she wouldn't have recognized Cole Rayburn in a million years.

Behind her own stinging eyes exploded a word she wouldn't dare say in front of her father.

"You've changed."

In more ways than you know, Cole thought, hyperaware of Bree's gaze on his profile as he focused on the kids, playing catch in the backyard with her dad. A steady, dark brown gaze that used to make his stomach turn somersaults a million years ago.

That still could, apparently.

He hadn't been able to read the emotions that'd streaked across her face when the penny dropped, although he'd caught the *What the hell?* easily enough.

Same goes, he'd wanted to say.

And for a moment, he'd considered gathering up the kids, getting out. Except the Colonel had given him a *Deal with it* look that brought an end to that idea. A look that the Colonel probably had been waiting a long time to give. Man had zero tolerance for unresolved issues. Especially involving his children. That the statute of limitations had long since run out on this one was beside the point.

Fiddling with a bottle of tea he didn't really want, Cole released a breath. "When I realized these kids might need me to stick around past fifty, I decided it was time to get off my butt. Start eating like a human instead of some garbage-munching bacteria."

"Or a teenage boy?"

"Same thing."

Her chuckle was subdued. "And the glasses…?"

"LASIK. Got tired of breaking my glasses, can't tolerate contacts."

From the yard, they heard her father laugh, the kids responding in kind. Cole wasn't sure who was blessing whom more. Right now, he didn't care.

"How old are they?" Sabrina said softly.

"Wesley's thirteen, Brooke twelve."

"Wow. You were…young."

Amazing, how normal their conversation sounded, considering the way they'd left things. "Not that young," Cole murmured, sitting forward, his hands clamped around the bottle.

He sensed more than saw her take a sip of her own tea.

"You with kids. Gonna take a minute to wrap my head around that. So where've you been all this time?"

"Philadelphia, mostly." Cole finally tilted his own bottle to his lips.

"And you're here now because…?"

"Here, as in Maple River? Or your dad's house?"

"Either. Both." At his silence, she added, "You're the last person I expected to see right now. So color me curious."

At that, he turned, starting slightly at the flashback— her sitting cross-legged on the cushioned wicker chair, her wavy hair cupping her shoulders. Even the skinny pants and loose top weren't much different from what she used to wear. But for the first time since he'd encountered her again, Cole got his head out of his butt long enough to see the pain etched in *her* expression. Masked, to be sure, but definitely there. And far more real than that pity-me shtick she used to pull in high school.

Real or not, however, no way was he going to get sucked in. Not this time. Or ever again. Those big brown eyes be damned. Not to mention all that luggage in the vestibule. Full plate and all that. So whatever was going on with Bree, he didn't need, or want, to know.

However, since he was on her turf, he supposed an explanation was in order.

His gaze shifted back to the kids, a smile tugging at his mouth when Wes—far more coordinated than Cole had been at that age—caught the ball. "The kids' mother and I have been divorced since they were babies," he said quietly. "Up to last week we had shared custody."

"Last week…?" Her breath hitched. "What happened?"

"The kids asked Erin to choose between them and her… personal life."

Several beats preceded "And she didn't choose them?"

The horror in her voice made him smile. As did the softly uttered, but very crude, word that followed when he shook his head.

"I can't imagine…" She blew out a harsh breath. "Sorry, I don't even know the woman—or your kids, for that matter—it's not my place to judge. But still."

"Yeah." When Bree didn't respond, he said, "The thing is, Erin and I… It was a mistake. Plain and simple. And if she hadn't gotten pregnant…"

"The first time or the second?"

Cole smirked. "We told ourselves it was working by then. We were wrong." He paused. "It took her a while longer to finally admit motherhood cramped her style."

At Sabrina's silence, he turned again to find her watching the kids with an intensity that sent a jolt of awareness through him. Finally she sighed, then said, "So you brought them back here."

Setting the bottle on a nearby table, Cole stood and walked over to the porch railing, his hands slammed into his jeans pockets. "For the summer, anyway. My folks needed someone to house-sit. And my sister and her family are here. It'll be good for them, having a break until we figure out what comes next."

"And you ran into Pop in the Food Lion. Amazing."

"I think that's called fate."

He heard her snort. "So their mother… She simply washed her hands of them?"

"They talk. Text." He looked at her. "It's only been a week. And she's still their mom."

Her downturned mouth—there was a familiar expression—made it clear what she thought of his assessment before she nodded toward the yard, where her dad was giving Wes pointers on how to throw the ball. "Looks like maybe they're helping each other."

"So I didn't imagine it," Cole said. "That he's lonely?"

Her cheeks puffed when she blew out a breath. "The others are around, of course. They get together a lot, he's hardly neglected. But it's not the same, from when the house was always filled."

Cole took another swallow of his tea. "Can't quite believe he's selling it."

"Not sure how hard, though. It's been on the market for months. And it's not overpriced, but…"

"He doesn't really want to leave."

The kids' laughter floated over to them from the far end of the yard. Her smile seemed halfhearted. Nothing like the sassy grin he remembered. "Can you blame him?"

Cole thought of all the kids who'd found sanctuary here, temporary or otherwise. Himself included. How Jeanne Noble's generosity, the Colonel's strength, still permeated the space. It was a good house, filled with good vibes. Mostly, anyway.

"No, I can't." He squinted. "So you don't mind? That we're here?"

"Why should I?"

For oh, so many reasons, he thought, then looked away again, annoyed that he was still having trouble staring directly at the girl he'd once loved so hard it'd scared the snot out of him. Sure, those feelings were gone, but the memory of them wasn't. And his fists clenched underneath his folded arms as the compassion in her eyes threatened to reopen not only newer, not-yet-completely scabbed over wounds, but much older ones he'd thought long since healed.

Then she got up to join him at the railing, and he shut his own eyes against the onslaught—of memories, of her scent, of disappointment and uncertainty and longing. Man, was he messed up, or what…?

"Dad tell you about Matt and Kelly?"

The amusement in her voice brought Cole's gaze to the side of her face again. "Kelly? McNeil?"

"Yep."

Back in school, Cole and Sabrina and Kelly had been—in hindsight—a very strange but very loyal triumvirate.

Until Kelly moved away their senior year, and everything… changed.

"Matt and Kelly, what?"

"Married, if you can believe it. New baby, even. Well, three months old now. Although she already had two kids from her previous marriage."

Cole's head spun. Sure, everyone knew Kelly'd had a crush on Bree's twin brother, but she'd been too shy to say anything. And Matt…well. Matt was Matt. Focused, one might say. Which was another word for oblivious.

"I don't… Wow."

Bree laughed. "Long story. Happy ending. Or beginning, I suppose. They don't live far. In case you run into them in the supermarket or whatever. But fair warning—they're ridiculously happy. It can grate, after a while."

This was said with such love—and obvious pain—Cole felt his gut twist.

"I can imagine."

A moment passed before she nodded toward the kids. "Tell me about them."

He got another whiff of her perfume, something far more sultry than the sweet, flowery scent she used to wear. The image of all that luggage piled in the foyer flashed through his brain, the tears shining in her eyes—

"Wes is scary smart," he said. "Especially in math. There was some talk about letting him skip a year, but I said no. Other kids already think he's a freak as it is."

"He gets picked on?"

A world of understanding packed into four words. "Enough." He hesitated, then said, "Nothing like I was, though. Thank God."

She flashed him a quick smile, then asked, "And Brooke?"

As usual, his heart softened when he looked at his daughter, tall and blonde and still blessedly shapeless—although for how long was anybody's guess. No longer a child, nowhere near being a woman…and Cole had no clue what to do with her. Except love her.

"Into dance, art, music. Science. Every bit as smart as Wes. And not even remotely interested in capitalizing on that."

"Because she's seen what's happened to her brother and doesn't want to go there."

"Maybe. Whatever. Drives me nuts."

"Give her time, she'll get over it."

Feeling his lips twitch, Cole looked over. "You sure?"

"I did," she said, then laughed. "About being myself, I mean. Mostly, anyway. But those hormone swarms are a bitch."

"Yeah. I remember," he said, and she laughed again, then gave him something close to a side-eye. "They'll be fine, Rayburn."

"Why would you say—"

"Because you're their dad." Not looking at him, she stuffed her fingers in her front pockets, the lightweight top scrunching over her wrists. "You were a good friend," she said softly. "A good *person*. Even if we messed things up—"

She cut herself off when her father appeared at the porch steps, leaning heavily on the bottom post and breathing hard.

"Pop? You okay?"

"Of course I'm okay," the Colonel said, swatting a hand at his daughter before hauling in another lungful of air. "You guys all keep reminding me I need more exercise, so I got it." Then to Cole, "You and the kids are welcome to stay for dinner. Easy enough to fire up the grill—"

"Thanks," Cole said. "But we're going to my sister's—"

"Right, right—I forgot."

At the mention of Diana, Cole saw something flash in Bree's eyes. The vestiges of fear, most likely. His sister, ten years his senior and Cole's self-appointed surrogate parent whenever his well-meaning but easily distracted academic parents dropped the ball—which was frequently—could definitely be scary.

"How is Diana?"

"Good. Bored, though, now that her two oldest are in college. Keeps making noises about going back to work. But anyway," he said as the kids tromped up the porch steps, looking a little flushed but otherwise none the worse for wear, "we should get going."

"C'n we get something to drink first?" Wes panted out.

"It's five blocks, you can't wait?"

The kid pantomimed clutching his throat, as if he'd been on a fifty-mile hike in the desert, and Bree smothered a laugh. Clearly eating it up, Wes grinned, then did his poor puppy dog face. "Man, I would kill for some Gatorade right now."

"There's tea and juice in the fridge," the Colonel said. "Help yourself. Although in my day," he said, shepherding them back inside, "we made do with drinking from the hose…"

Bree chuckled again as Cole's phone buzzed—a text from his sister, wondering where they were. "You really shouldn't encourage him," he said, pocketing the phone.

"Pop?"

"No. Wes. Kid's a master manipulator."

"Yeah, I seem to remember somebody else like that." She shoved her hair behind her ear. Flashed a smile. "This was nice, catching up."

"Sure."

Her eyes shadowed for a moment. "So…I'll be seeing you guys again?"

"Maybe." Because if he said *no*, then he'd have to explain why. And frankly, he wasn't sure he could. "How long are you staying?"

Although her smile stayed put, the shadow darkened. "Not sure—"

"Dad!" Brooke burst back on to the porch, holding out her phone. "Aunt Di says if we don't get over there *right now*—"

"You guys go on, tell her we're on our way."

But when he turned back around, Bree had wandered out into the yard to sit on one of the swings on the old play set, looking like the world's most lost little girl as she stared off into space.

And Cole stood there far longer than he should have, watching her.

Full plate, he reminded himself, then turned to leave, telling himself the image would fade.

Eventually.

Chapter Two

Her underwear dumped into the top drawer of her old dresser, Sabrina shoved it closed and sighed, missing Mom—who would have been right there with her, if not tucking things into drawers and hanging up stuff in the closet, at least sitting on the foot of the bed, listening, eyes soft with sympathy or bright with anger. Honestly— Sabrina zipped up the empty case and rammed it underneath the twin bed—more and more, her life felt like some artsy foreign film where bizarre crap kept happening but you had no idea why. And a happy ending was not a given. Chad used to drag her to those. And she'd go and pretend to enjoy them for his sake, but mostly she was just *Huh?*

Take the past twenty-four hours, for instance. As if having her future ripped from her in the space of a single conversation wasn't bad enough, then to run into Cole Rayburn, of all people. After which they'd had this perfectly normal, totally weird conversation, as though nothing had happened.

Okay, that wasn't entirely true. There'd definitely been some heavy-duty skirting of the truth going on. Some people might call that civilized and mature. Because it was ancient history and all that. Except…this was Cole and her.

For whatever that was worth.

Which would be not a whole lot, Sabrina thought, starting downstairs. Dude obviously had his hands full. And, yes, that was her heart squeezing inside her chest, especially when she thought about his kids…

She released another breath. Only so much multitasking her poor brain could handle right now.

Through the open patio door, the scent of charbroiled meat floated in from the deck where Pop was grilling. Stalling, she got a diet soda out of the French-door fridge in the recently remodeled kitchen, all stainless steel and sparkly white quartz and cherrywood cabinets. Very pretty. Still, she missed the homeyness of the old seventies decor, the knotty pine and faux brick, the old gouged table where they'd eaten, done homework, spilled their guts to Mom. Even the kids who'd only been passing through.

The family room, however, she thought, popping the can's tab as she peeked in the room, still bore the scars of having been a *family* room in every sense of the word. Probably one reason why the house was still on the market. The kitchen showed well, sure, but the rest of the house…not so much. Especially to buyers with no desire to take on a fixer-upper, even if most of the work was cosmetic. True, Pop had impulsively donated Mom's vast, and eclectic, book collection to the library some months before. But since he hadn't moved any further in that direction, Sabrina could only assume—since they'd never discussed it—that the action had paralyzed him instead of propelling him forward.

She tilted the can to her lips, remembering the beehive of activity this house had once been, of noisy meals and fights for the bathroom and never-ending chore lists, usually overseen by the man currently grilling their dinner.

Now only an eerie stillness remained, a thousand memories whispering like ghosts every time Sabrina returned. For all she'd chomped at the bit to escape more than a decade before, seeing it this way—like a dying person halfway between this world and the next—made her very sad.

Sadder, anyway.

The can clutched to her chest, she finally went outside, smiling for her father.

"Smells great."

Standing at the grill, Pop glanced over, then said, "All unpacked?"

"Mmm-hmm."

"Good," he said, not looking at her, and her eyes filled. Because all she wanted, she realized, was a hug.

Dumb.

She'd wondered sometimes, how, with their polar opposite natures, her parents had ever gotten together. Let alone enjoyed the kind of marriage that textbooks could point to and say, *This.* Mom had been the one who'd wrap Sabrina in her warm embrace, doing all the talking for both of them during those first few weeks after she and Matt had arrived and Sabrina wouldn't, or couldn't, find her words. The Colonel, however, hadn't seemed to know what to do with the frightened little girl clinging to her grief like a tattered teddy bear. Oh, Sabrina eventually figured out that, despite his more reserved nature, Pop cared fiercely about every child in his care, that fostering had been his idea. There was no better man on earth. But sometimes Sabrina felt as if their initial interaction—or lack of one—had set the tone for their entire relationship.

That even after all these years, she still had no idea how to close the gap between them.

"Got some vegetable kebabs from the store to go with the burgers," he said. "That okay?"

"Sure."

Fragrant smoke billowed out when he lifted the lid to

the grill, frowning again in her direction. "Sorry to spring Cole and the kids on you like that. If I'd known you were coming—"

"No, it's okay. I should've warned you."

Pop had known, of course, that things had fallen apart between her and Cole their senior year. Just not why. God willing, he never would.

"Always did like that boy," Pop now said, flipping the burgers. "Missed him hanging around."

"So you ran into him and invited him over."

Shooting her another curious look, Pop closed the lid to the grill again. "For more than five years that kid was over here more than he was at his own house. Seemed like it, anyway. Invitation was out of my mouth before I even knew it was there." He crossed his arms. "Couple of smart kids he's got there."

"So Cole said," Sabrina said, walking to the edge of the deck jutting out into the large yard off the porch. Shards of dying, early evening sun sliced through the pine trees on one side of the yard, gilding the new grass and her mother's prodigiously blooming rosebushes. A robin darted, stopped, darted again across the lawn, ignoring the chattering of an unseen squirrel nearby. Images flashed, of badminton and croquet games, of running through the sprinklers. That old Slip 'N Slide. Fireflies. Of lying in the grass on summer evenings, her and Cole and Kelly…

"You gonna go see the baby tonight?"

Releasing a breath, Sabrina turned, bracing her hands on the deck railing behind her and refusing to feel sorry for herself, that Matt was married and her younger brother, Tyler, was going to be in a week, that even her oldest brother, Ethan, had found love again after losing his wife three years ago. That things seemed to be working out fine for everyone but her.

Not that she hadn't tried—

Okay, maybe that not-feeling-sorry-for-herself thing wasn't working as well as she'd hoped.

"Tomorrow, maybe. It'll be too late after dinner. They'll be wanting to get the little one down, I imagine."

Her father shoved his hands in his pants pockets. "So you gonna tell me what happened, or are we playing twenty questions?"

Sabrina smirked. "Wondered when you were going to ask."

"Didn't want to push."

She held up her left hand, naked except for the imprint of the ring that had been there only yesterday. "Not that you haven't already figured it out."

"It was his boy, wasn't it?"

Her vision blurred, Sabrina nodded. Chad didn't have his six-year-old son very often—his ex had moved to the West Coast for work, and Robbie went with her—meaning the child wanted Daddy to himself when he did see him. Not that Sabrina blamed him.

"I couldn't stand seeing the kid so miserable, Pop."

"So you broke it off."

"It was a mutual decision."

"And the child was six. He would have gotten over it."

From anyone else, her father's words might have sounded callous. Uncaring. Except Sabrina knew the remark came from a place of deep love for kids. All kids. Which only made it harder to hear.

"You think I gave up."

She nearly choked when her father walked over, wrapped her in his arms. For maybe two seconds, but still. Holy crap.

He let her go to return to the grill, scraping burgers on to a nearby plate before giving her a hard stare. "I wasn't there, I have no idea what went on between you. But I know *you*," he said, jabbing the spatula in her direction. "I know how good you are with kids. How crazy they are about you. So whatever was going on…" He lowered the lid again. "Not your fault."

"Yeah, well, you also never liked Chad."

"Only because I never felt he was worthy of you."

"*What?* You never said that—"

"Didn't have to, did I?"

"Chad's a good man, Pop. Jeez, give me some credit." He slanted a look in her direction, and her face warmed. "My point is, this wasn't about me and Chad, it was about me and his little boy—"

"And that was his father's issue to address, not yours. And if he couldn't, or wouldn't, do that…" His eyes narrowed. "Did he even try to fix the problem?"

"To be honest…" Her mouth twisted. "He looked… relieved."

He jabbed the spatula at her again. *Point made.* "Sounds to me like he's the one who gave up. You also have no idea what the kid's mother was putting in his head about you."

Actually, considering some of the things the child had said to her, she had a pretty good idea. But no need to add fuel to that fire.

Pop's gaze softened. Marginally. "All I want is for you to be happy. Trust me, wouldn't have happened for you with that guy. Not in the long run. Because eventually you would have lost out to the kid. Which you obviously knew, or you wouldn't have ended it. Right?"

You know, there was a reason she'd left home. And not only because small-town Jersey was suffocating her. That the man spoke the truth—yet again—was beside the point.

Pop plated the kebabs, setting both them and the burgers on the table. "So I take it you're staying for a while?"

"A few weeks, maybe," Sabrina said, sitting across from him and spearing the smallest burger. "Until I…get my bearings again. That okay?"

"Like you have to ask. As long as I still have the house, anyway." He glanced over again. "No bun?"

"Carbs, Pop."

Shaking his head, he took a bite of his own burger, his gaze drifting out to the yard. Sabrina could probably guess what he was thinking. Or rather, who he was thinking about. Not looking at Pop, she slowly pulled off a piece of pineapple from her skewer and asked, "You ever think about dating again?"

After a long moment, she looked up to meet his glare. *Bingo.*

"And what would be the point of that?"

"Oh, I don't know. How's about going to a movie or out to dinner with someone not related to you? Might be fun. You should try it."

One side of his mouth pulled up. Sort of. "This you not wanting to whine about your own problems?"

"You bet. So?"

Her father took another bite of his burger. "Seems like it'd be more trouble than it's worth. Especially at my age."

"So what're you going to do with the next twenty or thirty years, Methuselah? Watch TV all day?"

"And maybe after all those years of taking care of everybody else, all I *want* to do is watch TV."

"Not buying it. Sorry."

"I'm good with things the way they are, thank you. Once I get out of this house…"

His voice once more trailing off, Pop glanced around, almost as if he didn't recognize the place, before facing Sabrina again…and she saw in his eyes the depth of his loss in a way she never had before, prompting her to lean over to lay her hand on his wrist. Pushing out a sigh, Pop covered her hand with his own.

"You know, I lost track of how many times we moved, when I was on active duty. The number of places we lived. Far as I was concerned they were only places to sleep, way stations between assignments. But this…" He looked around again. "This was home. Where we raised all you kids. I know I don't need it anymore. Have known for some time. And I plunked down my deposit on a one-bedroom unit at Sunridge last month—"

"Really? I didn't know that."

"Nobody does. Didn't want you all hounding me."

"Pop. *You* decided to sell. Months ago—"

"And at the time, I thought I was good with that decision. And in here," he said, tapping his head, "I still am." Then he palmed his heart. "In here is another story."

"Which is why, I assume, you're dragging your heels about giving the place a face-lift."

"Jeannie picked out every paint color, every stick of furniture in the place. What somebody does with it after I'm gone is none of my concern. But as long as I'm still here, it's *my* home. And damned if I'm going to spend whatever time I have left in the house feeling like I'm in somebody else's."

"So why'd you redo the kitchen?"

He huffed a breath through his nose. "Because even I had to admit it was falling apart. Half the drawers didn't even close anymore. And the old range was down to two functioning burners. So I caved, let some kitchen designer convince me that an upgrade would add value to the house."

"I'm sure it did."

"Except I hate it. Looks like a damn showroom. Or a commercial kitchen. Not like someplace a family wants to hang out. Frankly, I'd change it all back if I could. Except they tell me you can't even get those green appliances anymore."

"And thank God for that," Sabrina said, and her father humphed. "Pop…you need to make a decision here. A real one, I mean, not this half-assed thing. Otherwise you're wasting both the Realtor's time and yours. If you don't want to sell, then don't. I mean it," she said at her father's startled look. "Take the place off the market, tell Sunridge you changed your mind—"

"And forfeit my deposit?"

"If it comes down to that, yes. For heaven's sake—for once in your life, go with your gut, not only your head. If it doesn't feel right to leave, don't. It's your house, your life. Your right to reverse course. But don't move forward with something only to save face, or because that's what everyone's expecting—"

Her gaze lowered, her uneaten food a blur. She felt her father's touch on her wrist, as gentle-rough as his words. "Why do I get the feeling we're not talking about me anymore?"

She jerked her hand away, even as she laughed. Hyena-esque though it may have been. Because she had seen the writing on the wall with Chad. Like neon-hued graffiti, actually. But in spite of the troubles with Robbie, she'd clung to the relationship for far longer than she should have. Because she was so, so tired of...

Of failing.

"Hey," she said, smiling. "You're the one who can't decide whether to sell his house or not."

But after she'd retreated once more to the room that still bore the scars of her youth—a hundred tiny pushpin pricks from long-gone posters, a red stain on the windowsill where a candle had melted and overflowed—the cold, hard truth came right with her, that she'd fallen into the very trap she'd sworn to avoid.

Of letting desperation make a fool of her.

Exactly like she had with Cole, all those years ago.

She hurled her old teddy bear across the room, where it bounced off the closet door with a pathetic little squeak.

"So Sabrina's back?" Cole's sister said, stretching plastic wrap over the leftover salad.

Yeah, he wondered how long it'd take before she brought up that particular subject. Figuring it best to jump the gun before the kids said something at dinner, he'd casually mentioned she'd been at the Colonel's.

"Yep," Cole said, warring with himself about having a second piece of chocolate cake. With caramel filling. Sitting there on the counter, taunting him like some barely clad sex kitten in an X-rated dream. Squelching a sigh, he looked back at Diana, while in the family room beyond, her youngest and Cole's two were watching some zombie flick, the expressions on their faces not a whole lot different than the characters on the screen. "Visiting, or something. Had no idea she was going to be there. Or she, us. What're the odds, right?"

"How is she?" Diana asked stiffly, and Cole smiled, even as he silently cussed out his brother-in-law for abandoning him to the she-wolf that was his sister. Some flimsy excuse about a crisis at his restaurant.

"Down, sis. That was a long time ago."

Her eyes cut to his, then away again when she turned to grab the cake cover and rattle it over the plate, hiding temptation. "Just asking."

Even though she'd been married and a mother already when it became obvious Bree was no longer a part of Cole's life—having been the center of it for so long—it was Diana who'd seen through his lousy attempt at stoicism and realized her baby brother was hurting. Never mind that he'd brought most of the pain on himself.

"We talked, Di. Watched the kids play with the Colonel. That's pretty much it. Hey," he said to the mother of all skeptical looks, "you remember that dude you dated your senior year? What was his name?"

Di frowned for a minute, then said, "You mean Stuart? Gosh—I haven't thought of him in years."

"But back then you two were pretty tight, as I recall."

He couldn't tell if Di was more shocked or amused. "You were *seven*, for pity's sake. How would you...?"

"I might've heard Mom and Dad talking. Sounding worried." He shrugged, enjoying his sister's blush. "So tell me—if you were to run into Stuart now, would you still feel anything?"

"What? No! Why would I?" Cole lifted an eyebrow, and his sister sighed. "One word—Andy. Who wiped all thoughts of other guys out of my head the minute I met him. Also, Stuart didn't break my heart."

"Bree didn't—"

"Cole. Please. Memory like a steel trap."

"Then how come you're not remembering that *I* broke it off?"

"Damage control doesn't count. And besides…" Her gaze gentled. "Then there was Erin."

She stopped there. Thank God. Although there would have been a time when she wouldn't have.

"Look," he said, "we ran into each other, we talked, she'll go back to New York and I'm here. With my kids." He glanced into the family room. "Speaking of damage control."

His sister leaned over to kiss him on top of his head. Like he was five, for God's sake. Then she looked into the family room, her mouth curved down at the corners.

"How are they doing?" She turned back to him. "And before you answer, I've survived three teenagers. My BS detector is top-of-the-line."

"You tell me. Since you watched them like a hawk all during dinner."

"This can't be easy on them, leaving Philly, their friends…"

"They're cool with it, you guys are three houses away and it's only for the summer."

"And then?"

"Haven't gotten that far."

"So you're not going back to Philly."

Not if I can help it, he thought, then smiled for his concerned sister. "Keeping our options open for now. Di—

it's been a week. Give us a second, okay? Although I am thinking—if we stay here—of putting them in Sedgefield."

That got another disapproving look. "Public school was good enough for us, as I recall."

"For some of us, maybe."

His sister sucked in a short breath. "Sorry—"

Cole held up a hand, cutting her off, then refolded his arms over his chest. "Sedgefield's a better fit for the kids than any of the middle schools here, I checked. And I can afford it." Which his parents hadn't been able to, not on their professors' salaries. For years, Cole had wondered how different things might have been, if he'd gone there. Although of course now he knew bullying could happen anywhere. And if he had, he wouldn't have met Sabrina...

Thereby saving himself a whole boatload of heartache.

"And they were already in private school in Philly, anyway," he said, seeing a mind-numbing, body-exhausting workout in his near future. Because if he dreamed about Sabrina tonight, he was a dead man. "Hey, sweetheart," he said when Brooke slogged into the kitchen and collapsed into his arms. He'd never thought of himself as the kind of daddy to actually *have* a daddy's girl, but what did he know? "Movie over?"

She shook her head. "But my eyeballs were about to fall out of my head, it was *so* disgusting. Why do boys like stuff like that?"

Diana chuckled. "A question I've been asking myself for years. Want another piece of cake?"

"Di—"

"Have you looked at your daughter recently? I swear she's grown two inches in the week since you guys got here. Kid needs fuel."

"And I did eat two helpings of veggies," Brooke said, all big green eyes. "*And* a salad—"

"Okay, okay," Cole said, laughing in spite of himself. And honestly, it wasn't as if either of his two showed the slightest indication of having the same weight issues that had plagued Cole for so long—equating food with comfort, as some sort of compensation for whatever he'd believed was missing from his life. His own parents had turned a blind eye, for reasons Cole would never understand. But damned if he was going to do the same thing.

While Brooke downed her second piece of cake and the boys finished up the movie, Diana packed up enough food to last them until fall.

"You know," Cole said, the bulging bag knocking against his thigh as they walked outside and the kids raced ahead "I really hate it when you pity me."

"That's not pity, it's looove." Cole groaned; his sister laughed before giving him a one-armed hug. "I've missed you, twerp."

"Yeah. Me, too." And amazingly enough, he meant it.

Brooke let out a shriek at something Wes said to her, and Diana chuckled again. "They're going to be fine, honey," she said softly. "And so will you."

"I am fine, Di."

She gave him one of her looks. "No, you're not. And don't argue with me, I know you a helluva lot better than you know yourself. You need someone, Cole."

Yep. Still the same pain in the ass as ever.

"I have someone. Two someones, in fact."

"Not what I mean, and you know it." She paused. "I didn't regret for one minute my decision to stay home with the boys. But if Andy hadn't been there, too…" Cole could feel her gaze on the side of his face. "Raising kids is hard. Raising them on your own—"

"Is not beyond the realm of possibility." Bemused, Cole lowered his eyes to his sister's. "And if you even try to fix me up, I will kill you."

She laughed. "Not to worry. Every woman I know who's even reasonably the right age is either married, insane or a skank. Sometimes all three."

"You need new friends."

"Tell me about it. But you need—" she rubbed his arm, her voice gentling "—to put yourself out there, sweetie. And don't give me any flak about having the kids full-time. Because they're always welcome here while you—" her mouth twitched "—search."

Smirking, Cole ignored the headache trying desperately to take hold. His sister meant well, she really did. But even if he had the time—or energy—to pursue a relationship, right now was about the kids' needs. Not his. Because damned if he was going to do to them what their mother had.

"Thanks for the offer, but we're good."

Then he hotfooted it down the walk before she could regroup. A talent at which Diana excelled.

Despite his aching head—which the kids' near-constant bickering behind him for the past ten minutes hadn't helped—Cole smiled for the trio of wriggling, curly-tongued pugs swarming Brooke and Wes when they got back to his parents' house.

"Let 'em out," he said, dumping his keys on the same little dish on the table by the front door that had been there forever, as the beasts raced through the modest bungalow and through the now-open patio door. Cole quickly unloaded the bag of food, stuffing what needed to be refrigerated into the old white side-by-side before joining kids and dogs outside.

The yard wasn't particularly large, but it backed onto a wooded parcel separating the neighborhood from a secondary highway. Dimly, Cole could hear that same hum of traffic that used to lull him to sleep at night as a kid, that had served as a comforting backdrop to now-forgotten conversations.

Maybe not so forgotten.

Expelling a breath, he shoved his hands into his pockets as he stood on the cement patio, willing the almost-cool evening breeze to unclog his brain, relax the muscles strangling the base of his skull.

Ironically, his sister's prodding about the future—the one she saw for him, anyway—had only jerked awake another scene from his past, of a scrawny sixth-grade girl who'd had no trouble verbally smacking down that trio of bullies, all twice her size, who'd been making Cole's life a living hell. Trying to, anyway. Since in reality their ass-hattery hadn't bothered him nearly as much as it apparently had her.

His mouth curved in spite of himself as he remembered the good times, of how natural and easy things had been between them.

Until an influx of rowdy hormones drowned out every ounce of intelligence and common sense Cole had possessed, blinding him to who, or what, Sabrina had become—

"Dad? You okay?"

He hadn't even realized Wes had plopped into one of the patio chairs, long legs stretched in front of him, his pant hems hovering north of his ankles. A trip to the mall was in order, Cole thought, suppressing a shudder. "Sure."

"Really? Because you've been, I don't know. Weird."

Out in the yard, Brooke threw a ratty old tennis ball for the dogs, laughing when they all tripped over each other trying to get it. Smiling, Cole crossed the patio to sink into the chair next to Wes's, then leaned forward to link his hands between his knees. "Hey. Weird is my middle name."

The kid snorted a laugh through his nose. "Okay, weird*er*. Seriously, on the way back from Aunt Di's? You didn't even tell Brooke and me to stop messing with each other."

"And you're complaining?"

"I'm… Well, no. I guess. But…" Something made a

peeping sound in the woods. Frog? Bug? "I thought you said you and Sabrina had been best friends?"

"We were." Brooke flopped on the grass in the fading light, then writhed in laughter as all three dogs assaulted her with sloppy kisses. "Actually, she saved my butt when we were kids. Thinks she did, anyway. Took on a bunch of bullies who apparently took issue with the way I looked."

"Took on? As in, beat them up or something?"

Cole laughed. "Bree's a lot tougher than she looks, but… no. Read 'em the riot act, though. And pointed out her twin brother, who was easily twice her size. And theirs. But like I said, we hadn't seen each other in years. And I certainly wasn't expecting to see her today. Or her, me." He glanced over at his son. A breeze ruffled the kid's too-long hair, almost as curly as Cole's. He looked back out over the yard. "So it was definitely strange."

"So, what? You guys just hung out together and stuff? You didn't date?"

"No," Cole said mildly. Truthfully. Although with a slight, if insistent, pinch to his chest. "We spent most of our time at the Colonel's. But sometimes here. Where it was a lot quieter."

"Quieter?"

"The Colonel and his wife Jeanne had adopted four kids—including Sabrina and her twin brother—and then had a baby of their own right about the time Bree and I met, in middle school. Add to that everybody's friends… place was definitely hopping."

"And Mom couldn't even handle two kids," Wes muttered, and Cole's gaze snapped back to his son. He'd given Bree a severely edited version of the story, of course. Partly because he was hardly going to air his—or, in this case, his ex's—dirty laundry to someone he hadn't seen in almost twenty years. But partly because he was ashamed, truth be told, that he hadn't made it his business to find out what exactly had been going on. Then again, how would he have known, if the kids didn't tell him?

But in the past few days, the truth had leaked out bit by bit, how often Erin would leave them on their own, or forget to pick them up, or even when she was there, retreat to her room and computer rather than interacting with her own children. He'd assumed, since she'd fought for primary custody, they'd be her priority. Instead, they'd apparently been so far down the list they were barely on her register.

His eyes burning, Cole reached over to clamp his hand around the back of his son's neck. God knew Cole was still jerking awake at night, heart pounding at the realization that no one was coming to get them on Sunday. That he was *it*. At the same time, no one was ever *going* to take them away, either. Ever again. Or leave them alone, or ignore them, or let anything—or anyone—come between them.

"All in the past now, buddy," he whispered. "Not that I know how to handle you guys, either—" that got a chuckle "—but we'll figure it out together."

Wes straightened up, his cool gray gaze far too trenchant for thirteen. "You make it sound like this is all new to you. We were with you almost every weekend—"

"This is different," Cole said. "This is…real."

"And forever?"

Cole's throat clogged again. "Yeah."

The boy stared at him for a long moment, then suddenly, and awkwardly, launched himself into Cole's arms to give him a sweaty, slightly funky hug.

And Cole thought that this was all he could want. Or need. Or, as his son so succinctly put it, handle.

Wes pulled free, scrubbing a hand through his hair. "C'n I go play on the computer for a little while?" He grinned. "I'm on level sixty-four."

"No kidding?"

"Yep. Nobody else in school—my old school, I mean—was even close."

"Huh. Clearly I didn't make it hard enough."

"Oh, it's plenty hard, believe me," Wes said, his cheeks dimpling. "Can't help it if I'm a genius."

"Well, genius, only for an hour. It's already late. You guys need to be in bed."

His son made a face, but he knew better than to argue. The bedtime rules—at least with Cole—had been set in stone from the time they were babies. And yet, they'd still wanted to come live with him.

After Wes went inside, Cole settled back in his chair, watching his daughter. It'd become a game, over the past few days, to see who'd run out of steam first—her or the dogs. So far, the dogs had won, every time. Lots of energy packed into those squat little bodies—

His phone rang. He dug it out of his pants pocket, frowning at the unfamiliar number.

"Cole here—"

"Yeah, so your sister said," a familiar voice barked in his ear. "Not that you'd bothered to tell *me*."

"I was going to call you tomorrow, I swear," he said, and the old woman snorted. Loudly. Aunt Lizzie had always been his mother's favorite aunt, hovering around ninety and with an attitude befitting a former Rockette who'd once "dated," or so the story went, someone high up in New York politics. After years of fighting the family about giving up her house in town, a broken hip two years before had finally convinced her to move into a retirement community, where she'd been blissfully raising hell ever since.

"So I need a favor," she said, as though it hadn't been months since they'd talked.

Cole's brows arched. Fiercely independent, Lizzie rarely asked for anything from anyone. One of the reasons Cole hadn't seen her was because she'd made it clear ages ago she didn't want anyone clinging to her any more than she wanted to cling to them.

"Oh?"

"Yeah. This friend of mine up here at Sunridge, she invited all of us to come to her granddaughter's wedding next Saturday. When I asked your sister a couple weeks ago she said she'd take me, so I wouldn't have to ride that god-awful community bus with all the old biddies. So I call her a couple minutes ago to make sure she remembers, and what does she say? That she totally forgot, she and Andy are taking George up to Adelphi that day to tour the place. Can you believe that sweet little boy is going to *college* next year? Damn, I'm getting old. But anyway. She said I should call you. So here I am. Calling. Can you take me?"

Cole smiled. "Don't see why not. But I've got the kids—"

"For the weekend?"

"No," he said quietly. "For good."

Silence. Then, "And you were planning on telling me this, when?"

"Tomorrow. When I called. It's a brand-new development, Lizzie," he said when she snorted again.

"So bring 'em. Anybody can come to the ceremony. And that way I'll get to see them. 'Cause it's been a while, you know."

"Hey. Not my fault you were on a cruise the last time they were here."

"Okay, you might have a point. Although remind me to never let Myrtle Steinberg talk me into going anywhere with her again. Alaska was pretty and all, but not exactly rife with hot young men in Speedos—"

"So who are these people?" Cole said before the discussion got worse. Which, with Lizzie, was a foregone conclusion. "The ones getting married?"

"What? Oh. Well, like I said, my friend's granddaughter. Laurel. Lovely girl, brings her baby boy when she comes to visit. Adorable, both of them. She's marrying one of the Noble boys, actually. The youngest one, I think. You still keep up with that Sabrina?"

Cole's heart knocked against his ribs. "How on earth

would you remember Sabrina? You only met her once. At graduation."

"Once before that, too. When I was still living over on Edgewood. You'd brought over a cake or something your sister had made, and Sabrina was with you. You don't remember that?"

"Um...sure?"

Lizzie snorted. "And they say old people are the ones with the sketchy memories—"

Panting, Brooke tromped over to the patio, collapsing into the same chair recently vacated by her brother. She frowned, pointing to her ear. Cole held up one hand as Lizzie repeated her question. Because one did not evade Lizzie.

"So you two still keep up?" she asked.

"Actually...I saw her today. First time since graduation."

"Get out. So what's she up to?"

"I don't know, really. She didn't say. She's been living in New York, though."

"No fooling? Good for her. Sure, I'm okay with living out here now, I'm old as dirt. Who the hell needs to fight those crowds anymore? Not me, that's for sure. But to be young and living in the city..." He heard her sigh. "But you say she's back?"

"Visiting, apparently. Because the rest of her family is still here."

"So I suppose she'll be there. At the wedding?"

"I...imagine so."

"Then I'll get to see her. She still cute?"

Cole laughed in spite of himself. "She's the same age as me, Lizzie. Thirty-five."

"And I'm ninety-one next birthday. And still cute as a damn button. Although why buttons are supposed to be cute, I have no idea. Okay, gotta go scope out a good spot for the movie before all the good chairs are taken, I'll see you on Saturday. The wedding's at two, but pick me up at one-fifteen, I want to get a good seat in the church. And dress nice, for God's sake, I got an image to keep up!"

"Dad? What was that all about?"

His phone pocketed, Cole turned to his daughter. "Your grandmother's aunt Lizzie asked me to take her to a wedding on Saturday. Meaning you guys get to go, too." He frowned. "Do you even have a dress?"

A look of utter horror flashed in his daughter's eyes. "I have to wear a *dress*?"

Just shoot him now.

Chapter Three

As Cole drove through the retirement community gates to pick up his aunt, the kids merrily bickering behind him, he grumpily acknowledged that it was a perfect day for a wedding: bright blue sky, puffy clouds, the barest breath of a breeze set at exactly the right temperature.

Unlike his own wedding day, which had been marked by miserably cold, torrential rains, the tail end of some far-reaching hurricane. Not that it would have mattered, the ceremony being a justice-of-the-peace affair with only their immediate families in attendance. Because neither he nor Erin had wanted a fuss. As if getting married was no big deal. Like buying a couch.

Except, looking back, they'd probably discussed the pros and cons of Ikea over Pottery Barn far more than they had whether or not to make things legal between them.

He still had the couch. Ikea. Erin's choice, and Cole pretty much hated it, but she hadn't wanted it when they broke up, and the thought of buying another one made

Cole's brain hurt. So there it was, along with the rest of the crap from his apartment, in storage. Although even he had to admit, after more than a dozen years of food spills, ground-in city dirt and more than a few unidentifiable stains, he supposed he should really think about buying a new one. Couldn't be any worse than dress shopping with his daughter, right?

Mercifully, the kids called a cease-fire as he drove around to Lizzie's apartment, a ground-floor unit with a courtyard view.

"I'll go get her," Wes said, bounding out of the car and up the short walk before Cole could ask, the beginnings of a swagger evident even though the kid's legs hadn't yet acclimated to his growth spurt. Of course, that might have had something to do with his "cool" outfit, all of the kid's choosing—khakis, designer sneakers, untucked dress shirt with preppy tie. Cole released a sigh, relieved that the boy seemed to be getting his mental feet under him again, at least, even if not his virtual ones.

Lizzie popped through her apartment door the instant Wes knocked, all dolled up in something flowery and floaty Cole vaguely remembered from his sister's wedding twenty years before. But with a floppy yellow hat and gold ballet slippers to complete the look. And jewelry. Lots and lots of jewelry, dangling and jangling as she made remarkably fast tracks toward the car, jabbing her cane into the sidewalk so hard he half expected to see sparks.

Wes scurried up from behind to open the car door for her, earning him a squeal of delight and a pat on the cheek. Even if she had to reach up a foot to do it.

"Such a good boy!" she said, carefully arranging sticklike limbs as she lowered herself inside, giving off enough mothball scent to fell a horse. "So rare to see good manners these days. Thank you, honey," she said to Wes when he climbed back into his seat. Then, as Cole backed out of the parking space, she twisted around to smile for Brooke, letting out a little gasp of delight. "And don't you look pretty, sweetheart! Is that a new dress?"

"Yeah."

"What's the matter? You don't like it?"

"It's okay, I guess."

Chuckling, Lizzie turned back around. "Tough customer," she muttered over the soft whirr of the car's air-conditioning, and Cole thought, with a smile, *You should know.* He'd seen pictures of his aunt in her glory days, the stunning blue-eyed redhead who'd lived, with five other girls, in a two-bedroom Brooklyn walk-up through the war. So Lizzie definitely knew tough. And now, even though a maze of wrinkles obliterated the dimples she'd said she'd always hated because they'd made her look like a kid, nothing was gonna dull the mischievous spark in her eyes. Or the joy.

Brooke could do a lot worse than to take after the old gal.

"What an absolutely gorgeous day," she said as they headed toward the church on the other side of town, closer to his old neighborhood. Behind them, both kids plugged into their phones, probably playing games. Cole couldn't decide whether to be annoyed or relieved. "It's funny," Lizzie went on, "how as you grow older you learn to appreciate all the crap you took for granted when you were younger. Like pretty days." She poked his arm. "And weddings."

Cole grunted. Weddings. Yeah. Not his favorite thing. Especially weddings where Sabrina Noble would be present—

"So what are you up to these days?" Lizzie said. "Still messing around with all that computer stuff?"

"Same old, same old," Cole said, grateful for the subject switch, even as he mentally shook his head at his aunt's take on his work. Although he supposed "messing around with all that computer stuff" was how it appeared to most people. Hell, there were plenty of times it seemed pretty trivial to him, too…until he opened his monthly statement from his investment broker.

"I've seen some of the people here playing that game on their whaddyacallits, those little flat TV screens you carry around?"

"Tablets?"

"Right. Those things. Or their phones. Your mother tried to convince me I needed one, but really, where do I go that I need to carry a phone around with me?" She let out a cackle. "The laundry room?"

Fortunately, she easily kept up both their sides of the conversation for the rest of the way to the church—a lovely, nineteenth century stone relic, built in a time when most of the then-predominately Catholic community went to mass every Sunday. To someone whose only church experience had been the occasional visit to the Quaker meeting house downtown, All Saints felt ridiculously overdone. Until he got inside, where a syrupy light filtered through jewel-toned stained glass windows, and giant ceiling fans gently hustled air pleasantly thick with the scent of flowers and ancient, much-polished wood.

Both kids were suitably awestruck. "It's really pretty in here," Brooke whispered, taking Cole's hand. Ahead of them, Lizzie clung to Wes's elbow, chattering a mile a minute, her voice ricocheting off the rafters. Amazingly, his son didn't seem to mind. Brooke giggled, then gave Cole a sheepish smile.

"I'm glad I'm wearing a dress."

Smiling, Cole squeezed her hand. "So'm I. Even though it's scary."

Pale blond brows scrunched at him. "Why?"

"Because you look way too grown-up in it." He shuddered, which got another giggle. Because she was still his little girl. At least for the next five minutes.

They slid into a pew, the wood smooth as glass. "I forget," Lizzie said around the kids, sitting between them, "how peaceful old churches are."

In theory, Cole thought as he caught a glimpse, through all the hats and hair, of Sabrina near the front, trying to keep a wriggling baby—a boy, he guessed, judging from his little blue outfit—from launching out of her arms. Beside her sat a younger woman, with another, younger baby, who was sound asleep. With a start Cole realized the tiny blonde must be Sabrina's baby sister Abby, whom Cole hadn't seen since she was five or six.

Then, because he was clearly a masochist, his gaze drifted back to Sabrina. Damn, she was gorgeous, her dark hair loosely piled on top of her head, a pair of dangly silver earrings grazing easily the most beautiful neck in the world—

"Dad? You okay?"

Cole smiled for his son, even as he thought, *Dude. Get a grip.* "Why do you keep asking me that?"

"Aren't the flowers pretty?" Lizzie said, nodding in obvious approval at the simple floral displays on the altar, large cut-glass vases overflowing with branches of mock orange blossoms. "That's her grandmother's doing, I'll bet my life on it. We have a million of those bushes on the property. She probably got them from there. Absolutely gorgeous. Oh! Isn't that Sabrina? Sitting down there with the family? My goodness—she hasn't changed a bit, has she?"

Physically? Maybe not. He doubted she'd gained five pounds since he'd last seen her. But the pretty teenager he remembered had nothing on the fully ripened woman sitting twenty feet away, her smile—as she kept up a conversation with the babbling baby on her lap—twisting his heart even more than it had the other night.

A heart he didn't dare let be twisted. Not now, not by anyone...but especially not by Bree.

Some guy in official, churchly garb appeared in front of the altar, along with a good-looking blond dude wearing the standard nervous/happy look of the about-to-be-wed—Sabrina's younger brother Tyler, obviously. And that could only be Bree's brother Matt beside him, darker and broader and more imposing than ever. The processional began, starting off with an adorable, curly-headed tot in a frilly white dress scattering rose petals, closely followed by a boy of maybe nine or ten whose chief job was apparently to keep the little girl on track. Next down the aisle was a stunning redhead—an almost unrecognizable Kelly, radiating confidence. Joy. Cole smiled, genuinely pleased for her. Then everyone stood for the bride, a trembling, sparkly-eyed brunette in a poofy, pale pink gown that threatened to swallow up the much older woman walking her down the aisle.

"That's Marian," Lizzie whispered across the kids, loudly enough that everyone in front of and behind them could hear. "Laurel's grandmother. Isn't that sweet? And don't they both look gorgeous…?"

But Cole wasn't paying attention, because he was once again watching Bree as she kissed the baby's head, only to stifle a laugh when an eager little hand clutched a fistful of hair and tried to stuff it in his mouth.

Too late, Cole wrenched his gaze away. Because the sweetness of the scene was now wrapped every bit as tightly around his heart as the baby's hand in Bree's hair.

The good news was, at least once the wedding was over and he'd delivered Lizzie back home, they were done. Since he was hardly going to crash a wedding reception, was he?

Even before he reached Kelly in the reception line, she let out a squeal loud enough to make Matt flinch beside her. Not to mention the groom, who almost fumbled the baby in his arms. The baby, Cole realized, Bree had been holding.

"Ohmygod!" Kelly shrieked, her hand flying to her mouth. *"Cole?"*

So much for the shy, mousy girl who, when they were

in school together, seemed quite content to drift in the
wake of Sabrina's effervescence—much like Cole had, he
thought on a sigh as the maid of honor yanked him into a
fierce hug, her wild red curls tickling his nose.

"This is *crazy*!" she said, holding him apart. "Holy moly,
you look amazing, I almost didn't recognize you! What
are you doing here? When did you get back? *Why* are you
back? And are these your kids?"

"Honey?" Matt said on a chuckle beside her, even as
Cole wondered why Bree hadn't told her. "There's like a
thousand people behind him. Catch up later." This said
while Matt clasped Cole's hand in a firm handshake, a
hundred questions in his dark brown eyes. "Dude. Last
person I expected to see."

Even though they were in the same year, they hadn't
been even remotely close in high school. Different crowds,
different tracks. But being Bree's twin, Matt had obviously
been aware of how tight Cole and Bree had been. Although
hopefully not *that* aware.

"Last place I expected to be, believe me," Cole said with
what he prayed came across as an easy smile...the smile of
a guy who no longer had to worry about this guy ripping his
head off his shoulders. He hoped, anyway. "Small world."

Letting go of Cole's hand, Matt laughed. "To say the
least."

A proud Lizzie usurped Cole's shot at introducing his
offspring to the wedding party, and it amused Cole to see
Wes trot out actual social skills, to watch Brooke go all
goofy at the sight of the baby.

After hugs all around, Cole reached for Lizzie's elbow to
escort her down the church steps, the kids going on ahead.
But they'd no sooner reached the sidewalk when Kelly
caught up to them, her green eyes glittering.

"You guys are coming to the reception, right? I mean,
if you have to take Lizzie back, anyway—"

"Oh. Um...we didn't exactly get an invitation."

She laughed. "I'm in charge of the food. Trust me, there will be enough to feed half the state. So you'd hardly be imposing." Her eyes softened. "You were part of this family, too, Cole. Same as me." Her attention swung to the kids, laughing at something Lizzie said, then back to him. "And we'd love to get to know the kids better."

At that moment, Sabrina emerged from the church, carefully balancing the frilly-dressed baby her sister had been holding as she navigated the steps. Someone he didn't know stopped to admire the infant; smiling, Bree shifted the baby for the woman to get a better look, laughing at whatever she said.

"That one's ours," Kelly said softly, and Cole looked back at her. "Matt's and my new daughter. Three months old last week."

Cole grinned. "Congratulations. Name?"

"Teresa Jeannette, after Matt's and Sabrina's birth mother. And Jeanne, of course." Her nose wrinkled. "We're kind of crazy about her."

"No. Really?"

Kelly chuckled, then sighed. "Bree's holding it together pretty well, don't you think? I mean, considering."

"Considering?"

At what must have been his puzzled expression, she flushed. "Oh, right…you don't know. Look, forget I said anything—"

"Too late, Kell. Considering *what*?"

Kelly glanced over at Bree, then back at Cole. "She was supposed to get married in a few weeks," she said in a low voice. "But the wedding got called off. That's why she's back—"

"Honey?" Matt called down to her, his forehead crumpled as he lifted his hands.

"Be right there!" she called, standing on tiptoe to buss Cole's cheek, whispering, "But you didn't hear it from me!"

before gathering her long skirt and running back up the stairs to her husband.

Well, that would definitely explain the pain he'd seen in Bree's eyes that day. Not to mention the deadly mixture of sympathy and self-preservation now threatening to choke him when her gaze bounced off his, that bright smile momentarily faltering before she yanked her attention elsewhere.

Mercifully breaking the pull that, whether he wanted to admit it or not, was still there. Even after all this time.

Even though it made no earthly sense.

"So there's a party, too?" Brooke now said in front of him, all bright eyes and wonder, and Cole wondered how it was his children had been around for more than a dozen years and never attended a wedding. Or, apparently, even heard of the tradition. "Aunt Lizzie says it's gonna be awesome, with tons of food and everything."

Yeah. Everything. Including a boatload of emotional... stuff he didn't want or need to deal with right now. If ever.

Lizzie clamped her hands on his daughter's shoulders from behind, her I've-seen-it-all gaze locked in Cole's. "Everyone's invited," she said softly. Well, softly for Lizzie. "And the kids are already dressed so nice." Her eyes narrowed. "And it's not as if you have anyplace else to be, is it?"

How about hell? Cole thought, resigning himself to the inevitable.

Wiggling a Coke can in sweaty fingers, Wesley frowned through the open French doors toward the grassy area past the pool, where Dad's old friend was sitting on a bench. Alone. Weird. Except, considering how noisy and hot and crammed with old people this room was, maybe not so much—

"So go talk to her," his sister said beside him, making

him jerk. "Before you stare a hole through her or some-thing."

"I'm not staring," he muttered, deliberately twisting around and lifting the can to his mouth.

"Are, too. Were, anyway." Brooke took a noisy slurp of her punch, something bright pink and disgustingly sweet and probably lethal. "Not that I blame you. I'd like to know what the deal is, too."

"So why don't *you* go find out what's up?"

Brooke glanced over her shoulder, then back at the mill-ing crowd, her cheeks getting all splotchy. "Because I'd have no idea what to say? You're the one who can talk to like, anybody. Me..." She shrugged.

Which was probably why she'd made Wes talk to Mom. Not that he hadn't been thinking, too, how crappy things had gotten, with the boyfriends always coming and going, the way Mom always seemed distracted. Like she had other things she'd rather be doing than hanging out with her kids. It'd been making Wes nuts for a long time. But he hadn't said anything to his sister because *she* hadn't, and he didn't want to upset her.

Neither of them had really thought Mom would make the choice she did. But she had. Like, without even think-ing about it for two seconds.

Wes glanced across the room at Dad, talking to some dude a little older than him, maybe, standing with a cou-ple of boys about his and Brooke's age. Sabrina's oldest brother, Ethan, and two of his kids, Wes remembered. Dad looked over, giving him a *You okay?* look. Wes nodded. Sometimes it felt like Dad cared almost too much. But after Mom? He'd take it.

He smiled, thinking about that first night after they'd come to live with Dad for good, and he'd come right out and said they'd have to be patient with him, because there was a huge difference between being the weekend parent and being the only parent, and that he honestly had no idea what he was doing. Pretty much the same thing he'd said the other night, actually, after they got back from the Colonel's. Although why Dad thought that, Wes had no idea. Since he obviously had it together a lot better than Mom did.

Then this Sabrina person appeared…

"He says they were friends," he said, swallowing hard. "When they were in school. No big deal."

Brooke didn't look convinced. "I don't know, the way he keeps looking at her…"

"And you've been reading too many of those sappy books."

"*Jane Eyre* is not a 'sappy' book, moron. And it's better than playing those stupid video games all the time—"

"Like the ones Dad designs, you mean?"

Brooke blew out a cherry-scented sigh. "It's just, after Mom…"

"I know. But Dad already said—"

"Oh, and like grown-ups never say whatever they *think* you want to hear?"

"So why wouldn't she do the same thing?" Wes said, nodding toward Sabrina.

His sister's mouth got all squinchy, as if maybe he had a point. But then she looked back at him with those big eyes of hers and said, "Please?"

One thing about Brooke, she never whined. Well, hardly ever. And she wasn't now. But he could see the worry on her face, that they'd barely solved one problem and here was another one, knocking on their door. Because they'd seen it over and over, not only with Mom, but with other kids they knew with single parents—the minute a new adult appeared on the scene, the kids got shoved to the back of the line. Okay, maybe that wasn't totally fair; he could think of a couple of times where it worked out okay.

But only a couple.

Wes glanced outside again, thinking, wouldn't it be nice, for once, to not have to worry about the grown-up stuff?

To simply be a kid? Seriously, even if they didn't know where they were going to live after the summer yet, or go to school, things at least felt more or less normal. Finally. Because Dad…he really was there for them. Also, he was cool with being the grown-up. No matter what he said. Meaning Wes could already tell getting to live with Dad full-time was the single most awesome thing that had ever happened to them.

And no way was Wes going to let that get messed up.

"Will you be okay?" he said to Brooke. "While I'm gone?"

"I've got my e-reader, I'll find someplace to read—"

"No, don't do that—Dad'll freak if he doesn't know where you are. Go hang with Lizzie. Or that girl over there—the one with the long hair, who talked to us earlier? Sabrina's niece, I think?"

His sister pulled a face. "I don't know…"

"She seems really nice, Brookie. See? She's smiling at us."

After a moment, Brooke sighed. "Okay."

"Good." Wes handed his sister his empty Coke can. "Then, I'll go see what I can find out."

She looked so relieved Wes's chest hurt.

"How come you're out here all by yourself?"

Half curled up on a bench underneath a lushly leafed apple tree, Sabrina jerked her head around, forcing a smile for Cole's son. Thank goodness she hadn't been crying. Not that she hadn't come close, more than once. But she'd rip out her eyeballs before that happened. Especially at her brother's wedding, for pity's sake.

No surprise, really, Cole's ending up at the wedding. Because that's how things worked in small towns. Forget *six* degrees of separation. Two, three max, and boom. Tight.

But now her heart knocked at the sight of this kid whose silver eyes—not to mention his perplexed expression—

hurled her straight back to the sixth grade and another set of silver eyes. Another perplexed expression. Both of which had made her breath hitch when she'd spotted them at the church.

"And how come you're not over there enjoying the party?" she said lightly.

"Because it's boring?" Wesley said, plunking down on the bench beside her, his long legs stretched out in front of him. Already taller than she was, Sabrina noted. Not that this was saying much. But at this rate he'd pass his dad's height before he finished middle school.

"There's a few kids around your age. My brother Ethan's twins—"

"Don't know 'em."

"You don't know *me*," Sabrina said gently.

One side of his mouth lifted—another Cole-ism, heaven help her—before he looked up through the tree's branches, heavy with tiny green fruit.

"At least it's cooler out here," he said, and Sabrina smiled.

"Very true."

Still frowning, Wesley lowered his gaze to Sabrina's. Direct. Slightly unnerving. "Dad said you two were best friends when you were kids?"

Her pulse tripped. "We were. Did…did he talk about me, after you guys left the other night?"

Nodding, the boy looked away, the breeze ruffling his too-long hair. An approaching storm, maybe. In more ways than one, Sabrina thought with a mental grimace. "He said you saved his butt."

She had to laugh. "I'm not sure how much I saved your father's butt as I kicked some other kids'—although not literally, I'm no She-Ra—"

"Who?"

"Never mind," Sabrina said, waving her hand. "But, yeah, we were close. Then, I mean."

"So, what happened?"

Her elbow propped on the back of the bench, she leaned her cheek against her knuckles. "We grew up? Went our separate ways? That's what happens with most childhood friendships. Especially if you don't hang around. And why are you asking me this?"

"So you weren't, like, boyfriend and girlfriend?"

"No," Sabrina said softly. Because it was the truth. Despite what had happened. And no way was she going to be that honest, especially to a thirteen-year-old boy. "Did your dad say we were?"

"No. But…"

His foot started bouncing up and down as he swept a hunk of hair out of his eyes, and Sabrina ached for him, even if she didn't completely understand why.

"Things working out okay? Living with your dad?"

His eyes narrowing, the kid lifted his chin, his jaw tightening. "Dad's cool."

"I'll bet."

The boy's gaze slid to hers. "You were his friend, don't you remember?"

Sabrina smiled. "Nobody was a better friend than your dad. But 'cool' is not a word I would use to describe him then. Nerdy, yes," she said on a chuckle, and the corners of the boy's mouth twitched. "And before the other night, remember, we hadn't seen each other in nearly twenty years. People change."

"I guess." Wesley licked his lips. "He…tell you why we're living with him?"

"Yes." She paused, praying for the right words. "I'm sorry. For what it's worth, I got mad, when he told me. But to be fair, I don't know your mom. What her reasons were for her decision—"

"You're *sticking up* for her?"

"God, no. But it's not my place to judge her, either." Never mind that the look on the kid's face made Sabrina want to smack the woman senseless. Not to mention immediately regret even getting into it with the boy.

Wesley scrubbed one palm over his knee, then crossed his arms high on his chest. As though he were the one being cross-examined. "At least now…" His nose flared as he hauled in a breath. "At least Dad wants us. And it feels good to know—" she saw his baby Adam's apple bobble before his gaze slammed into hers, blasting her with every ounce of courage she imagined the poor kid could muster "—that we come first in his life."

It was everything Sabrina could do not to laugh. At the irony, the déjà vu, the universe's sick sense of humor… whatever. Except Wesley's completely justified concern went far deeper than a spoiled six-year-old's hissy fits. That his concern had no foundation in reality was beside the point. "Honey…I'm no threat to what you guys have with your dad. If that's what's worrying you."

"You sure?"

"Positive."

He looked away again, twin dots of color blooming in his cheeks. "I—we—just don't want things to get messed up. Again."

"I'm sure you don't," she said, her chest aching. "But don't you think you should be talking to your dad about this? Not me?"

His gaze bounced off hers, only to scuttle away. "All he'll say is that nothing's wrong. Or that we're imagining things. Crap like that."

"You don't trust him to be honest with you?"

That got another half-assed shrug. Only, as much as Sabrina wanted to refute the kid's paranoia or distrust or whatever—because she couldn't imagine Cole ever deliberately being dishonest with anyone, let alone his own kids—truth be told, there were a million reasons why people weren't always up-front with those they loved, and not all of those reasons were bad. In fact, most of them weren't.

And besides, how would she know what was going on inside Cole's head? She barely knew what was going on inside hers.

But she knew enough to say, "I think maybe what you're seeing is…uncertainty. That we're not really sure what we are to each other anymore. But believe me, I'm not looking to start—or restart—anything with your dad. For my own reasons, okay? I'm not saying we might not be friends, although even that would only be temporary, but that's all it would ever be. Because I'm not sticking around," she said to his frown. "I have a career in New York I need to get back to."

"Oh."

"Yeah. So you can tell your sister no worries, okay?"

"How did you—"

Now she did laugh. "My twin brother, Matt, was always very protective of me, too. Especially after our parents died, when we were little. So I'm really good at spotting the signs."

With a grimace, the kid turned around…only to flinch, which made Sabrina look up.

To see Cole not even ten feet away, practically radiating *What the hell?*

Chapter Four

"**D**ad!" The blush spread across his son's cheeks like wildfire. "I didn't see you there."

"So I gathered," Cole said quietly. "Now go rescue your sister before Lizzie talks her ears off."

His face still red, the boy pushed himself to his feet, barely enduring Cole's one-armed hug before striding off across the grass. Cole watched him for a moment, then turned back to Sabrina, thinking he might've found the situation amusing if he hadn't known how much his son was hurting. As was the woman in front of him, almost delicate in a wispy, pale blue dress that looked like something straight out of *The Great Gatsby*. Definitely not the sharp-tongued dynamo who'd never think twice about sacrificing her own safety in order to right a wrong. She would've made an awesome addition to the Justice League—a five-foot-two spitfire in a bodysuit and cape. And boots with four-inch heels. Oh, yeah—

Man. Clearly the heat was getting to him. Not to mention

the crowd. He'd never been a party person under the best of circumstances, even in college. The noise, the rampant violation of personal space, the futility of trying to engage in anything even remotely resembling meaningful conversation…not his thing. Funny, though, how with Bree he'd never felt that sense of suffocation, that he could be with her and still feel alone. At peace.

In the old days, anyway.

"I'm almost afraid to ask what that was all about," Cole said, and she laughed. After a fashion.

"I'm almost afraid to tell you."

On a tight smile, Cole hitched up the knees of his khakis and lowered himself to the bench beside her. "But you're going to," he said, not looking at her. Unable to.

She laughed again, the sound as gentle as the early summer breeze dancing around them. "I was being grilled." When Cole's head swung to hers, she shrugged. "He was curious, understandably enough. About what we used to be to each other." She paused. "What we might be now. Especially since you apparently told him I saved your butt?"

Grimacing, Cole looked away again. "And what did you say?"

"That whatever we once were," she said softly, "it's in the past."

Her words should have been a relief. Which they were, in a way. Then, why the sting? The stupid, totally illogical disappointment?

"He brought up what happened with his mom. Sort of. But it was obvious he was making sure I wasn't a threat."

Cole frowned at her again, even as he thought, *How could you ever be a threat? To anybody?* "To them?"

"More to…what the three of you have, I think. Or are just beginning to get hold of, maybe? In any case…" She flicked some tiny insect or other off her lap, then curled her hands around the edge of the bench. "Even if you were, well, in the market? I'm definitely not. So it's all moot."

Nodding, Cole looked away again. "Kelly told me."

"About?"

"Why you're here. Besides for the wedding, I mean."

"Ah."

He glanced at her profile. Or more to the point, the grimace tugging at her mouth. Too late, he remembered Kelly's parting remark. Damn. "I wasn't supposed to say anything, but—"

"No, it's okay," she said on a sigh. "Not exactly a secret."

"I'm sorry."

Bree squinted across the pool, then shrugged. "At some point I'm sure I'll realize it was for the best, but right now..." She turned the grimace on him, her dark eyes dry but flat. Nothing like the girl who used to rant and rave when some loser or other had done her wrong, her emotions hurtling from her tiny frame like Zeus's thunderbolts. "Sucks."

"Wanna talk about it?"

She looked as startled as he felt, the laugh practically exploding from her throat. "After everything..." Then she shook her head, her expression a cross between amusement and pity. "Really?"

"Old habits die hard?"

"Yeah. Like banging your own head against the wall, over and over. Or something equally self-destructive." When he frowned at her, she sighed. "I did eventually figure out a thing or six. Although, considering recent history, maybe not as much as I'd like to believe." She waved one hand in front of her face, as though dismissing the thought. "But I wouldn't blame you one bit for being cautious. For still hating me—"

"I never hated you, Bree."

She blew a soft laugh through her nose. "Sure not how it felt at the time."

Cole stared hard at his hands for a moment, then released

a breath of his own. "It was more that…I didn't understand what had happened."

"Join the club," she muttered, then sighed. "But still. I wouldn't have called you crazy. For hating me. Especially after the way I took advantage of you. How I…hurt you."

He took a long moment. "What you don't understand was that I was never a victim. Especially not of you."

"Even at—"

"Especially at the end." He felt his mouth go tight again. "Like I was going to turn down your coming on to me?"

"Even though I was using you to soothe my own ego after Jerry What's-His-Face dumped me."

And there it was, finally. In all its stinky, putrid glory.

"Yeah. Even though. It was still my choice. Like everything else in my life. Who I hung out with, what I wore, what I did, all of it. That's not to say I didn't have some major growing pains as a kid, like everybody else. That I didn't screw up. Or that life hasn't thrown in a monkey wrench from time to time. But how I've handled those monkey wrenches has been entirely up to me. So even then, I knew what I was getting into, even if I didn't know how to handle it." He paused. "Or what to do when it all blew up in my face."

Finally, he looked at her again, his chest aching at the obvious contrition in her expression. "But I'm not seventeen anymore. Meaning, if I ask you if you want to talk, I am fully aware of what I'm asking, why I'm asking and who I'm asking it of. Has nothing to do with bad habits from the past. But it does have everything to do with who I am now."

Their gazes tangled for a long moment before she said, "Which still doesn't explain why you give a damn about me."

He forced his attention across the pool, where Wes and Brooke were chatting with some of the other kids, all those Noble nieces and nephews that hadn't existed before.

"And believe me, the logical side of my brain is doing a serious *What the hell?* number on me right now. Because frankly, if we'd left things the way they were the other night—a onetime meet up, no biggie—that would have been the end of it. Then I see you in the church, and then my kid goes and talks to you, and…"

Cole sagged back against the bench before tightly crossing his arms over his chest. "The most important thing I learned from your family," he said quietly, "from *you*—was that human beings were supposed to be there for each other. To help each other out, even when it's maybe not convenient. Or easy. That putting other people ahead of yourself makes you a stronger person. A better person. And I want my kids to have that example."

"Except…if you never said anything, they'd never know."

"I would, though. And that's what counts."

"So this has nothing to do with me?"

Cole hesitated, then said, "I still care, Bree. Because what we had for so long trumps what we ended up with."

"But…?"

The smile in her voice made him sigh. "But gotta be honest—there's no way I'll ever again let anyone get to me the way you did. Yeah, I know," he said to her frown, "I said I made choices. And I did. Doesn't mean I'd make the same ones now. It's like you said to Wes—nobody's looking to get anything started again. For all the reasons we've already stated and probably a hundred more we haven't thought of yet. But since fate has thrown us together, anyway, why not take advantage of it and finally make things right between us?" He looked back at his kids, smiling when Brooke glanced over at him, seeking reassurance. "Or at least lay them to rest."

Staring at Cole's rock-hard jaw, Sabrina wondered why, if closure was what Cole was after—understandable enough, all things considered—would he invite her to do the one thing that'd gotten them in so much trouble in the first place? Although…maybe letting her dump on him was exactly what he needed in order to find that closure. You know, reminding him of why things had ended badly to begin with?

"You sure you want to hear this?"

He gave her a side-eye. Another skill he'd picked up in the intervening years. "You know about Erin. Fair exchange."

All righty, then. So she told him about Robbie, how Chad's son had never accepted her, no matter how hard she tried. How much she'd wanted him to like her.

"And yes," she said, failure bitter in her mouth, "I realize that given enough time, maybe he would have eventually come around. Not a risk I was willing to take. Although—"

This she hadn't told anybody. Not Kelly, not Pop. And certainly not her brother. As if, before, saying the words out loud would give them power. Weight. Now that it was moot, however…

"Although to be honest," she said quietly, "things hadn't felt right between Chad and me for some time. Even when Robbie wasn't around."

There was a long silence before he asked, "Got any idea why?"

Slowly, she shook her head, the bitterness spreading to her chest. "Too many expectations, maybe? Wanting it to work too badly? Who knows?" Her eyes stung, but only for a moment. "When I finally admitted I wasn't sure, Chad didn't seem all that surprised." Her mouth twisted. "Or upset."

"Damn. That's rough."

"Although he was very nice about it. Told me to keep the ring, to stay in the condo as long as I needed—I'd given up my apartment when we got engaged, moved in with him. Said he'd commute from his folks' place in Oyster Bay. But why would I do that? Keep a ring from a broken engagement? Stay at my ex's, for heaven's sake?"

"So you came home."

"To regroup, yeah." No point in telling him about the money issues. None of his concern. "I'm still in the city several times a week for appointments, but otherwise…" She shrugged. "So that's the story. And yes, there are moments I want to rip out my spleen with a grapefruit spoon. But they pass—"

"Come and get it!" Matt yelled from the community room's doorway. With a short chuckle, Bree shook her head.

"We really ooze class, don't we?" she said, getting to her feet and gently shaking out her filmy dress. "Guess we better hustle before they eat up all the food. Those old ladies are fierce, I tell you."

Cole stood, as well. "You ready for this?"

Her forehead pinched again, she lifted her face to his. "Why wouldn't I be?"

"I don't really have to spell it out, do I?"

Sabrina couldn't decide if it was comforting or scary as hell that, after nearly twenty years, he could still so easily, and so accurately, read her mind.

She tried another smile. "A wedding definitely wouldn't have been my activity of choice today. But that doesn't mean I'm not thrilled for my brother and new sister-in-law. And I should probably let everyone see I'm okay. Thanks, though," she said, walking backwards, suddenly needing space. Air. Her brain back. "For listening."

"Sure thing," Cole said, his eyes pinned to hers, and Sabrina had to fight the urge not to turn and sprint across the grass like a demon was on her heels.

For the next hour or so she lost track of Cole as she gamely navigated the shoals of a Jersey wedding reception heavily populated with tipsy guests over seventy, her sole glass of white wine clutched in a death grip. She'd picked at her food—as usual, Kelly had knocked herself out—but her appetite had apparently flown the coop with her self-esteem. God willing, both would return sooner rather than later.

The toasts had made her smile and cry and feel impossibly *verklempt* even as she beamed for her little brother, his own grin endearingly sappy as he lifted his glass to his bride. Tyler was—or had been, anyway—the perennial kid, the goofball of the family, dodging responsibility as though it were the plague. That he should fall for the centered, focused, older Laurel—who sniffled all the way through the toast—was living proof that God gets a kick out of messing with His creation. Of working things out according to *His* plan, not humans'.

Something Sabrina was probably going to have to remind herself of a lot in the coming days.

Normally she was all about parties and crowds and chaos—there was a reason she loved living in New York—but today she felt stifled. So, once dinner was over, she slipped away again, out onto a largish sunroom she hadn't noticed before, overlooking another view of the grounds. The conglomeration of cushioned wicker and wrought iron made her smile, reminding her of the screened-in porch at her father's. Between the furnishings, her dress and the pair of ceiling fans desultorily stirring the still air, Sabrina felt as though she'd been transported back to the twenties—

A soft cough behind her made her spin around, her hand on her chest.

"Sorry," Brooke mumbled. Curled up on a floral-cushioned chaise, an e-reader on her lap, her rosy cheeks radiated her embarrassment. "Didn't mean to scare you."

"You didn't." Sabrina smiled. "I didn't know anyone was out here. I can leave—"

"No, that's okay. I was thinking about going back inside, anyway."

"Really?"

A tiny smile flickered across the girl's mouth. "No."

"Your dad know where you are?"

She nodded. "He knows I have trouble dealing with a lot of people at once. He said he was like that, when he was a kid."

"I remember."

"You do?"

"Oh, yeah," Sabrina said on a soft laugh. "I was exactly the opposite. I always wanted to be doing something, be out with other kids. In fact, I hated being by myself back then. Your dad, though..." Smiling, she sat on the edge of a nearby chair. "He at least was adaptable. He could hang at my house—which was always noisy and crazy—for hours. Then he'd go home and hide out in his basement, playing video games to decompress."

"He still does that," Brooke said. "But not usually until we're in bed." The girl gave Sabrina one of those hard stares, like her father, her brother. Except her eyes were more green. "Juliette says you help people pick out clothes?"

Juliette, her brother Ethan's talented, beautiful sixteen-year-old daughter, the oldest of this generation of Noble cousins and a self-appointed mother hen to them all. "I do. That's my job, in fact, in New York."

"She says you're really good."

Sabrina felt her lips curve. "Sounds like I need to put that girl on the payroll."

Brooke's eyes lowered, her cheeks reddening again. "Do you...ever help kids?"

The question caught Bree off guard. "Not usually. But I don't see why I couldn't. Why? Do you know someone who could use my services?"

Now the blush ratcheted up to blazing. "Me?"

So not what she'd expected. Especially after that little confab with her brother. Although, judging from the girl's apparent inability to meet Sabrina's eyes, she suspected there was more than a little conflict going on here. What with Sabrina being the enemy and all.

"Oh, yeah?"

Still not looking at her, Brooke plucked at her dress. Pink. Busy. All wrong for her. "The thing is, everybody thinks I don't care about clothes, but I do. Well, I do now, I didn't a few years ago. You know, when I was a little kid?" Her eyes lifted, only to immediately skitter away again. "Anyway, we wore uniforms at school, so it was no big deal. But then I started seeing all these girls wearing stuff I liked, but I'm not sure it would look good on me?"

"What about your mom?"

The girl's mouth screwed to one side. "Not to sound mean or anything, but she dresses, well, kind of crazy. Not that I care how she dresses. Well, not too much. But she'd always pick out these things for me that…just, no."

Bree swallowed her chuckle. "Trust me, you sound like every kid on the planet. My mother—and I adored her—had no clue about current styles. We used to have screaming matches in Macy's. No lie," she said, smiling when, this time, the startled gaze held fast.

"But did she eventually let you choose your own stuff?"

"Let's say we learned to compromise. And sometimes she'd actually suggest something that didn't make me gag. Not that I'd ever give her the satisfaction, of course," she said, and Brooke smiled, only to then sigh.

"At least you guys went shopping together. With Mom… she'd simply come home with stuff. And if I said anything, about not liking it or whatever, she'd get all hurt."

Bree's heart cracked. Because nothing was worse when you were trying to figure out who you are than being forced to dress like someone you're not. "So you'd wear clothes you hated?"

"Pretty much. I tried to make them look cooler, but it never worked. And now that we're with Dad…" Her mouth pulled flat. "When we go to a store? He looks like he's gonna be sick or something."

At that, Sabrina released the laugh she'd been holding in. "Oh, sweetie—you should have seen some of the things your father put on his body when we were in school."

"I've seen pictures," the girl said, her mouth pulled to one side. "So sad."

Sabrina laughed again. "So whose idea was that dress?"

"Some saleslady in Bloomie's," she said, rolling her eyes.

"You don't like it?"

"It's a dress. Ergo, it sucks."

Ergo? Really? "What about your aunt? Couldn't she take you?"

"Um…she has boys? Why would she know anything about shopping for girls?"

"Because she is one?"

"Hello? She's ten years older than dad?" And hence, a throwback to the Paleolithic age. Got it. "So…would you take me?"

Moment of truth. Sabrina crossed her arms. "And does your brother know about this?"

The girl's forehead crumpled. "Huh?"

"Not an hour ago," she said gently, "Wesley made it very clear he wasn't comfortable with the idea of me—or anyone, really—coming between you guys and your dad. Not that I wouldn't love to take you shopping, but I do not want there to be any misunderstandings. And I definitely don't want your brother on my case," she added with a smile.

"Oh." Another blush stole across the girl's cheeks. "He, um, might have gone to talk to you because of me, actually."

Not as much as you might think, Sabrina thought, then said, "But then Juliette told you what I did, and you need to upgrade your wardrobe, so suddenly I'm not the enemy anymore."

Again, eyes lowered. Again, cheeks turned a lovely shade of crimson. "I guess that sounds sort of cruddy, huh?"

"Sort of, yeah."

Silence. Then, in a very, very small voice, she asked, "So you won't do it?"

"Didn't say that," Sabrina said, and Brooke's head popped up, expression all hopeful. "*But*, there are conditions. One, that your dad is okay with this. Two, that he coughs up sufficient cash to make the trip worthwhile." That got a grin and a giggle, and Sabrina's chest cramped. "And three," she said over the cramping, "that everyone is crystal clear that this is a one-shot deal and has nothing to do with your father and me. That work for you?"

In answer, the girl untangled herself from the chaise and launched into Sabrina's arms. Which she took as a yes.

Not to mention a challenge, she thought as she hugged the girl back.

One she fervently hoped her poor mangled heart was up to.

Chapter Five

Two days later, the engine to her father's SUV clicking as it cooled, Sabrina sat in the driveway to Cole's childhood home, letting her brain adjust to the intense déjà vu. Although they'd usually ended up at her house—because that's where the food was, he'd once said—she and Kelly had spent a fair amount of their waking hours here, too. And now those days came flooding back.

Because everything about the redbrick Colonial, a few blocks from the Colonel's, was exactly the same, down to the French-blue trim and white-paneled door, still flanked by a pair of neatly trimmed topiaries in sturdy stone planters. Unlike the Nobles' yard, which had always borne signs of the many children who lived inside—balls and scooters and bikes and such—no such detritus had ever dared litter the Rayburns' lawn. Then, as now, the grass was neatly mowed, all bushes painstakingly trimmed, the only flowers one small bed of white impatiens huddled against the mailbox post near the sidewalk.

Accompanied by a trio of wriggling pugs, Cole opened the front door. Reluctantly, Sabrina faced the muggy, mid-day Jersey heat. Not to mention much the same expression Cole had worn when Brooke had asked him if Sabrina could take her shopping. Because clearly immense relief at having someone else assume an obviously painful task was at war with...something.

"Your dad still does all this?" she asked, shutting the door—to the car, on that thought, whatever—as the pugs surged down the walk to swarm her calves, suspicion glinting in buggy eyes. Smiling, Sabrina knelt to let the dogs sniff her, their huffed breaths tickling her fingers.

"Oh, hell, no," Cole said. "Yard service, twice a month. Trim gets repainted every two years, same color." He hesitated, his hands plugged in his shorts' pockets as he watched the dogs, then finally lifted his gaze to hers. "I'm still not sure why you're doing this."

"Because I'm good at it and Brooke asked. And, yes, it really is that simple."

His gaze was unblinking. "You might find yourself reconsidering that statement after an afternoon with my daughter." When she laughed, the muscles around his mouth eased a little. "Well. You might as well come in. The kids aren't here yet. They spent the night with my sister—cripes, guys," he said to the dogs. "Give the woman room to move."

There'd always been pugs here, Sabrina remembered. Although clearly not these. "What are their names?"

"Larry, Curly and Moe."

Choking on her laugh, she looked up at Cole. Who hadn't gotten uglier since the wedding. Pity.

"You can thank my nephews for that. Mom was appalled, but Dad thought it was hysterical, so she gave in."

"Which one's which?"

"I have no idea. The kids swear there are differences,

but damned if I can see them. Not that it matters—call one, you get all three, anyway."

Sabrina eventually reached the front door, which Cole held open for her for a moment before heading toward the kitchen, the pugs prancing after him. "Am I hallucinating," she said, her heels catching slightly in the living room's silvery blue carpet as she followed, "or has absolutely nothing changed since we were teenagers?"

"Forget teenagers," Cole said from the other side of the mauve laminate breakfast bar. "Since way before that. I was too little, but my sister remembers... Um, can I get you something to drink?"

"No, I'm good, thanks."

"Anyway, Diana remembers how 'fresh' the pinks and blues felt after the rusts and putrid greens. She also remembers Mom's unequivocal declaration that she would never go through that again." He rubbed the back of his neck. "Apparently my parents nearly came to blows during the remodel. So now she refuses to change the colors, since if she did, she'd have to change everything else, and that ain't happening. In fact, I recently repainted the whole house. Well, maybe a couple of years ago now. The one and only summer the kids went to camp." At her raised brows, he sighed. "Erin's idea. They hated it. Not surprising, considering the one time I went I thought I'd been consigned to hell."

"But you let them go, anyway."

"Made them go is more accurate. Insisted they stay the whole month, too. Never mind that the tears nearly did me in. God, I felt like crap."

"Softie," Sabrina said, smiling, and Cole shrugged. But the love in his eyes...

She wrenched her gaze away from his, pretending a sudden and profound interest in the living room walls. "So. You actually painted this whole place by yourself?"

"I did. Kinda liked it, actually. You remember Kelly

and you and me painting your room when we were…what? Fourteen? That retina-searing bright pink?"

"It was called Cactus Flower," she said, meeting his grin with one of her own. "And you thought it was cool at the time."

"No, *you* did. Is it still that color?"

"Yes, believe it or not." She snorted. "Might be one reason why the house hasn't sold."

"Might be," Cole said, then crossed his arms. "Anyway…I like painting. Not a bad workout, and it leaves my mind free to come up with story ideas."

"For?"

"Video games."

"You're still doing that?"

"Now and then." The dogs *click-clicked* to the patio door, where they sat as one and gave Cole baleful glances over their shoulders. "Again? You just went." Somebody barked. "Fine," he said, unlocking, then tugging back the sliding glass door. "Go, pee. Live."

Much frantic shoving and pushing later, the dogs were outside. Cole lifted one hand. "Wanna join them?"

Sabrina's mouth twitched. "I'm good with the powder room, thanks."

"Oh, jeez—"

"Sorry, that was too good to pass up. And sure. Might as well wait outside as in here."

The backyard was exactly as she'd remembered, too—the sedate, verdigris iron furniture on the flagstone patio, the dogs snuffling around tidy flower beds with their regimented clusters of petunias and marigolds and dahlias, grouped by color. An engineer's garden, Cole had often said. Not flashy, but neat and orderly. The trees in the woods beyond the back wall were bigger, though, the heavy shade underneath their encroaching branches making the heat almost tolerable. She chuckled at two of the dogs playing tug-of-war with a rubber toy, while the third one pranced around them, yipping, wanting in on the action.

Sabrina and Cole stood a few feet apart, both watching the pugs, him with his hands low on his hips, her with her fingers slipped into the back pockets of her white cropped jeans. It was so strange: one moment it was as if no time had passed at all, the next they were strangers, the silences stiff and awkward.

"So when are the kids coming back...?"

"My sister texted me, they're running a little late. Sorry."

"No, it's okay." She paused. "It must feel strange, being here again. I mean, it does for me, whenever I'm at my dad's. Like I've time-warped."

"Tell me about it. Although I'm grateful for the option, that we didn't have to rush into buying something right away."

"Have you started looking?"

"Soon. Not another apartment, though. Someplace with a yard. That's really our own." He hesitated again, then said, "Until the kids came to live with me full-time I hadn't fully realized that I'd been in some kind of holding pattern. That we had. Not that I haven't been a hundred and ten percent committed to them, because I have, absolutely, but...it's hard to explain."

"It's okay, I get what you're saying."

His gaze touched hers. "Do you?"

"Enough." Then, sweeping her hair out of her face, she heard herself say, "You think you'll ever marry again?"

Because clearly the heat had melted her brain.

If it'd been anybody else asking the question—like, say, anyone related to him—Cole would have cringed. But this was simply Bree being Bree, spewing out whatever popped into her head. He sincerely doubted there was anything more to the question than idle curiosity.

"Right now? I doubt it. Especially since this is the first

chance we've ever had to be a full-time family, for the kids to have all my attention…" His shoulders bumped.

"What Wes said, in other words."

This stated as though fitting together the pieces in her head. His eyes grazed the side of her face. "I made a mess of my first marriage, Bree. Of all my relationships, frankly. In fact…" He looked away again. "The only relationships I haven't screwed up—at least not yet," he said with a wry smile, "are the ones with my kids. So might as well stick with what works, right?"

"At least you have that." Sabrina sighed out, then met Cole's puzzled frown with a slight smile. "Your kids, I mean. For years, all I wanted was a family of my own. And, not gonna lie, the ache's still there. But…" She pressed her lips together, shaking her head, before releasing a harsh sigh. "I used to think the only thing that really scared me was the idea of ending up alone. Now, though…"

"What?"

"Now I think what scares me most is feeling vulnerable. Weak. That if I'm not careful I'll end up like my mother. My birth mother, I mean."

Bree had never talked about her father's abuse until that summer before their senior year, of how—even though he'd apparently left Bree alone—he'd constantly ragged on her mother, on her brother Matt. Which is when it finally clicked why she hated bullies so much, what had prompted her to stand up for him on the playground when they were kids.

"Like that'll happen," he now said, and she smiled. "God, you were such a tough little thing in school. Like some warrior chick who wasn't about to take crap from anybody. In fact…" He weighed whether or not to tell her, decided what the hell? "You were the inspiration for more than one character in my games."

Her eyes bugged. "You serious?"

"Yep. Although—" he let his gaze flick to her chest,

then back up to her eyes "—I might have, ah, embellished things a little."

"Of course you did," she muttered, and he laughed. Then Sabrina sighed. "You do realize it was all fake, right? The tough chick act, not the boobs."

"Maybe," he said, and she pushed out another breath.

"Why on earth did you put up with me for so long?"

The regret in her voice sliced him in two. After a moment, he said, "Because I was blinded by the light glinting off the tough chick armor?" When she laughed, he added, not looking at her, "And then that armor would slip, and I'd see you were no different than me, really. And that was.... comforting, I suppose."

"In a very sick way."

"No arguments there. But those times, when you'd come to me…it was my chance to feel like the strong one. The more-together one. And that felt good."

Nearly twenty years, it'd taken him to find the strength to admit that. To himself, first. And now, to her.

"Really? My sob fests fed your ego?"

"Fed? Hell, kept it from starving."

"That is so sad," she said, her laugh soft as she shook her head. "On both our parts."

"Whatever works, right?"

"Until it didn't."

"No. Until it didn't."

"I'm so sorry," she said on a rush of air. "Really."

"Yeah. Me, too."

From out front, they heard the chaotic chatter of the kids' return, which sent the dogs into a yipping, wriggling frenzy. A minute later his sister shoved open the patio door and stepped outside, pale blue eyes glinting over high cheekbones as she gave Bree what she probably thought was a genuine smile.

"Brooke's gone to change, she'll be out in a minute. So. Sabrina Noble. My goodness. It's been…a while."

"Hey, can I get you anything?" Cole said, shooting his sister a *Be nice* glare.

"Thanks, but, no." Shoving her graying, left-to-its-own-devices hair off her forehead, Diana made a face. "I've got to haul my butt to the mall myself to start looking for an outfit to wear to that interview next week. Since soccer-mom chic won't cut it in the corporate world."

There was no disguising the terror in Di's voice. Currently attired in a polo shirt and skort combo—her uniform from April to October, when it was replaced by the same corduroy pants and pullover sweaters she'd been wearing since college—his tall, broad-shouldered sister had always had what their mother had diplomatically referred to as an "athletic" build. And, as with the rest of the family, absolutely no fashion sense. Or desire to accrue any.

"Got any idea what you're looking for?" Sabrina said kindly, and Di belted out a slightly hysterical laugh.

"You kidding? I've been a stay-at-home mom for twenty years. Seriously, other than the same black dress I've been trotting out for funerals for the last decade, and a blue one for weddings and Easter…I have no idea where to even start."

"Then, why don't you come with Sabrina and me, Aunt Di?" Brooke said from the patio door, making both women look toward the girl, all long hair and even longer legs, wearing a top and shorts that even Cole in his rampant cluelessness could tell was way too infantile for her.

"Oh, sweetie, I wouldn't want to interfere with your day," Di said, except Bree grinned and said, "That's a great idea!" and Cole thought *Please, God, no.*

His sister and Bree stared at each other for a good five seconds, the thoughts tumbling around in their heads perfectly obvious to everyone in the room except, he imagined, his daughter, before Bree said, "Seriously, I'm really good at multitasking. And trust me, I know where the bargains are."

At the word *bargains*, the corners of his sister's mouth curved up. "You don't say."

"Oh, but I do. Style is power, baby. But real power—" Bree's grin turned downright wicked "—lies in never paying full price for anything."

And that, apparently, did the trick. Broke the spell. Whatever. Because now his sister was looking at Bree much like Cinderella probably had her Fairy Godmother. But, frowning, she turned back to Brooke. "If you're sure—"

"It'll be fun, Aunt Di. Won't it, Sabrina?"

Bree chuckled. "Sure. Fair warning, though—expect to spend a lot of time in the dressing room."

His sister's forehead scrunched even more. "But you'll hand me things to put on, right?"

"Until you scream for mercy, yep. Let me go potty, and I'll catch up to you at the car..."

When she came back down the hall, however—and between her ponytail and those ridiculously hot white pants, damned if she didn't look at least ten years younger—Cole stopped her. "My daughter, I can understand. Maybe. But my sister? Why on earth—?"

"Because, atonement," Bree said softly, picking her purse up off from the floor where she'd dumped it earlier.

Cole felt his face warm. "I thought we agreed we were both guilty."

"Yeah, but I screwed up first. And maybe I feel like..." She glanced away, her mouth in a thin line, before looking back at him. "You know how there's paying it forward? Well, maybe I feel like I need to work backwards. Clean up a few old messes."

"You don't have to prove anything to me, Sabrina. And certainly not to my sister—"

"Maybe not. But I do have to prove something to myself. Or at least, do some good instead of wallowing. So, humor me, okay?"

After they drove off, Wes—in baggy shorts and a

scuzzy, tattered T-shirt that easily rivaled anything Cole would have worn at that age—came up beside Cole as he stood outside the still-open door.

"You sure that was a good idea?"

"It's a shopping trip, bud," Cole said, giving his son a brief smile. "Specifically, a shopping trip without either of us."

Wes nodded. "Good point."

But he could still feel the boy's tension. His wariness.

"She's only here for a few weeks," Cole said gently, refusing to acknowledge the pang accompanying the statement. "And whatever makes Brooke happy, right?"

That got a shrug. Considering the other options, Cole took it. "So. Just you and me, kid. What do you want to do? And be sure to pick something your sister hates."

After a moment, the kid grinned, then suggested the noisiest, crash-bangiest, most plotless flick currently playing.

"Perfect," Cole said, giving his son a high five, praying all those explosions would blast Sabrina Noble right out of his skull.

"I can't believe I'm about to say this," Cole's sister said as they trekked back to the SUV, their arms loaded with shopping bags, "but that was almost fun. Bargain hunting kicks *butt*."

Sabrina laughed. They'd been out for hours, and she could tell both Brooke and Diana were exhausted. But blissfully so. *Then my work here is done*, she thought, surprised at the flicker of disappointment the idea evoked. "Welcome to my world. You're both pretty much set through early fall, although you'll need to do this all over again come September."

Yanking open the back door to shove all the bags inside, Diana laughed at Brooke's groan. At Sabrina's suggestion, they'd hit up a nearby outlet mall, and both her charges had done her proud. Brooke, especially, had dutifully tried on every item Sabrina suggested, often gaping at her reflection in shocked delight.

"I'm starving," the girl now said, clicking her seat belt behind Sabrina.

"You and me both, baby," Diana said, then looked over at Sabrina. "How about you?"

"Don't you have to get home?"

"I texted Andy," she said as Sabrina pulled out on to the highway. "He and whatever boys are around will probably have pizza. They won't suffer, believe me. Hey," she said, nodding toward the glowing sign of a major chain restaurant, "will that work?"

"Do they have chicken fingers?" Brooke asked.

"I'm sure they do."

"Then, yeah. Okay."

Diana waited until the waitress had taken their orders and Brooke excused herself to go to the ladies' room before folding her hands in front of her on the table and spearing Sabrina with her periwinkle gaze.

And Sabrina thought, *Jeez, cookie...a little slow today, are we?*

Sure, she'd thought it odd earlier that Diana walked the kids back to Cole's when she lived all of three houses away, but it hadn't occurred to her until this very moment that the woman had actually finagled her way into tagging along on the shopping spree, for whatever purpose lay behind her *Gotcha now, bitch* expression.

Very clever. Scary as crap, but clever.

Taking a sip of her iced tea, Sabrina said, "You know, I had thought of suggesting you tweak your hair. But now I'm thinking that soft style really flatters your face. A trim, maybe, but definitely leave the silver. It'll make people take you more seriously—"

"Break any of their hearts, and your kneecaps are toast."

Slowly, Sabrina set down her tea. "And it took you four hours to say this?"

"Like I was going to risk pissing you off before you helped me with my wardrobe. But I mean it. They're all in a really tender place right now. Especially the kids. Do not mess with them."

The server brought them their salads. Sabrina drizzled her ranch dressing over the crisp greens before saying, "I know they are, Diana. And even if I didn't, I have no intention of 'messing' with anybody right now." At Diana's dubious expression, she sighed. "I was supposed to get married next month. My fiancé broke it off a couple of weeks ago."

"Oh. Damn."

"Yeah. So believe me, I'm feeling a little tender myself."

Across from her, Diana glanced over her shoulder, then leaned toward Sabrina and whispered, "Like you were back in high school?"

"Excuse me?"

"When the two of you—" she lowered her voice even more "—hooked up."

When Sabrina could breathe again, she said, "Cole *told* you that?"

"Not in so many words, no. And not right away. But when I kept nagging him about why you guys weren't hanging out anymore, he turned as red as that beer sign over there. Not unlike the color you are now. So I put two and two together."

"And came up with what, exactly? Since you more or less admitted you guys didn't actually *talk* about what happened, I'm guessing you missed the part about how he was the one who ended the relationship. You can ask him, if you don't believe me."

Diana continued the staring thing for several seconds. "So you're saying you didn't go nuts on him?"

"It was a lifetime ago, Diana. And whatever happened

between us, it was mutual." Her mouth flattened. "Stupid as hell, but mutual."

His sister stuffed a chunk of romaine lettuce in her mouth, then said around it, "Don't get me wrong," she said, "I had a great time this afternoon. I like you. I liked you then. Because I could see how good you were for my brother. Until—"

"Diana, jeez. Moot point, okay? Not to mention Cole's a big boy now. He doesn't need either of us to protect him anymore."

"It's the kids I'm more worried about."

Sabrina's fingers strangled her fork. "And even suggesting I'd ever hurt a child only goes to show how little you know me. And seriously—how ticked would Cole be if he knew we were even having this conversation? So back off. Now."

Finally, his sister cracked a smile. "And there's the Sabrina I remember."

"Yeah, well, ten years in New York haven't exactly mellowed me," she said, and now Diana laughed out loud, only to loudly exhale.

"I meddle because…well, you understand. Family. And our parents…" She sighed again. "It's not that they didn't care, but…"

"I know. I remember." Sabrina paused, then said, "Cole was very lucky to have you looking out for him."

"Except then I got married and moved away, and…" Diana's mouth flattened. "Professionally, Cole has done so well, it's scary. But personally…" Her head wagged. "And if anybody deserves good things, it's that kid. Okay, man," she said at Sabrina's frown. "Did he tell you? About the game?"

"*The* game? He did say something about still designing them, like as a hobby or something, but…what?"

Diana held up one finger, then twisted to pull her phone

from her purse, tapping the screen several times before handing it across the table. "You ever play this?"

"No, I'm not really into this stuff. But my nephews, absolutely, all the time—wait." Her eyes shot to Diana's. "This is *Cole's*?"

"Yep. He developed it about five years ago, almost as a joke, and it went viral." She took back her phone. "Fortunately, he took my advice and trademarked it first. Not only the game, but the characters, the 'worlds,' all of it. He thought I was nuts. Then. Now—" She grinned. "Not so much."

"Wait—so all the related toys and junk I see all over the place—"

"He gets licensing fees for. Yes, indeedy."

"Jeebus," Sabrina said, and Diana chuckled.

"Exactly. Who do you think sent Mom and Dad on that trip? Not Andy and me, that's for sure. Nor do they have to worry about retirement, even if they live to over a hundred. And Wes and Brooke will be able to go to any school they get into. The kid's no Bill Gates, but he's not hurting... Hey, honey," she said as Brooke returned, plopping down beside her aunt and smiling shyly at Sabrina as their entrees arrived. She could see nothing of Cole in the girl, with her green eyes and straight blond hair—unlike her brother, who reminded her so much of his father it was startling.

But what she could see, in that smile, in those eyes, curled up inside Sabrina like an affection-starved kitten... much like what she'd seen far too often in the eyes of too many fosters who'd passed through when she'd been a kid herself. That *What now?* look.

Will anybody ever love me enough?

To keep me?

To want me?

To not screw up?

Except, although Brooke and her brother had been hurt, they hadn't been abandoned. And never would be, not as long as Cole was around, she thought on a pang that nearly took her breath. Gosh, she doubted they even understood, at least not yet, or not fully, how incredibly fortunate they were to have their dad to pick up the pieces, to make them whole again.

To love them.

Sabrina, however, knew exactly how fortunate she was to have this strong, brave, *good* man in her life again.

Even if for only this single, precious moment.

At the flash of car lights in the picture window, Cole lifted his eyes from his e-reader as the dogs crowded around the front door, woofing and wriggling. Outside, car doors slammed over waves of women's laughter, his daughter's higher-pitched giggles—a sound that made him smile. He set the reader on the side table by his father's favorite chair, standing as the door opened and Sabrina and Brooke burst inside, practically invisible behind an army of shopping bags.

"You guys leave anything for anyone else?" he said, and Brooke giggled again, her face flushed. She was already wearing one of her new outfits—at least, Cole didn't recognize it—skinny black jeans with a filmy, sleeveless top with bunches of roses all over it. And sparkly black flats. They dumped the bags in the middle of the floor, sending the dogs into a sniffing frenzy.

"We might have gotten a little carried away," Sabrina said over the crackling and rustling as the dogs investigated, her gentle smile for his little girl punching him right in the gut. The same smile, he remembered, she used to give her baby sister. Or any other little kid, for that matter. Now she turned that smile on him and his heart cramped. "And you should see your sister's haul. No more mom jeans."

"Yeah, Aunt Di actually has a butt now. Where's Wes?"

Brooke asked, totally oblivious that her father had choked on his own spit.

"Next door. I think maybe he and that Keenan kid hit it off."

"Oh. That's nice. I guess."

You'll find friends, too, Cole wanted to say, even as he knew that would only make things worse. "So. This one of your new outfits?"

"Uh…yeah." Biting her lip, Brooke flashed a hesitant look at Sabrina before fingering her hair behind her ear. "Do you like it?"

"Turn around." She did, slowly, arms stiffly at her side, hands fisted, before meeting Cole's gaze again. And all he could think was—as every ounce of breath left his lungs, never to return—if she looked like this at twelve, scrub-faced and modestly attired, God help them all when she hit sixteen. Still, somehow, he smiled. "You look great, sweetheart."

"Really?"

"Really."

The girl released what sounded like a hugely relieved sigh, even as Sabrina said, "See? What'd I tell you? Gorgeous is gorgeous."

"Couldn't've said it better myself," Cole said, and Brooke flung herself into his arms to bury her face in his chest. His most excellent little surprise package, he thought, his eyes stinging. Then she pulled back, her own eyes bright.

"Wanna see what all else I got?"

"You bet. Fashion show, right here. Five minutes."

Her smile lighting up the room, Brooke pushed through the sea of snuffling dogs to gather up the bags, bump-bumping down the hall to her aunt's old bedroom, her canine companions close at her heels. Sabrina laughed, making Cole turn. And if he'd had any breath left, it would have beat a hasty retreat, too. Yes, even though her hair was a mess and her lipstick was eaten off and there was some sort of food splotch on the front of her blouse. Or maybe because of all of that. Because she was real.

Because she was Bree. Still.

"Thank you," he said, and she grinned at him.

"You kidding? We had a blast."

"So I gathered. And she looks…" He hesitated, searching for the right word. "So confident."

"Doesn't she? But that's the thing about clothes, when they showcase who you really are inside. Which ain't easy for a twelve-year-old, who has no idea who she is. Inside, outside, any side. Not a kid, by no means a woman…it's rough, that age."

"But you nailed it."

"We nailed it together. Although fair warning—some of the things she picked might seem a bit out there. To you, anyway."

"Hey. As long as she doesn't look like one of those *Real Housewives* chicks, I'm good."

Bree chuckled. "No worries. She wouldn't have gone for the slutty stuff, anyway. But still looking like she was ten wasn't cutting it, either." Her lips curved again. "Brooke's a great kid, Cole. And I loved being with her. Getting to know her."

Feeling his face prickle, Cole looked back down the hall, where he could hear, even through the closed door, some pop star warbling her heart out…and his daughter joining in. Amazing.

"She's never done that before. Sung like that, I mean. Not that I've heard, anyway."

"Oops." At his frown, Bree laughed. "One of the stores was playing nineties hits. I might have started singing along."

"Really? You still do that?"

"Every chance I get. Hey, don't knock it—some dude on the Lower East Side once handed me five bucks. No lie.

I'm thinking of playing Columbus Circle next. Could be a nice little second career, whaddya think?"

"I think if anyone could pull it off, it'd be you. So you and Diana…it was okay?"

"Besides her threatening to break my kneecaps if I hurt you or the kids? Sure."

"God, I'm sorry."

"Hey. Gotta give her props for loyalty, right?"

"Okay, here's this one…"

Brooke reappeared, this time wearing a short gray dress that hugged her slender waist, black sparkly leggings, a little jeans jacket and a giant, bright-colored scarf or something looped helter-skelter around her neck. Chuckling, Bree stepped over to readjust the scarf, working a magic in a few seconds that Cole wouldn't be able to accomplish in a lifetime.

"Wow," Brooke said to her reflection in the mirror next to the dining table, fingering the scarf as if she was afraid it would disappear. "Cool. But I'll never be able to make it look like this."

"It's not rocket science, sweetie. I will teach you all my tricks."

"Promise?" the girl said, looking at Bree in the mirror.

"Absolutely—"

The front door opened; Wes came in, stopping dead in his tracks when he spotted Bree before his gaze swung to his sister.

"What do you think?" Brooke said, twisting around, her eyes sparkling. "Sabrina helped me put this all together—"

"What the *heck* are those things on your legs? And that scarf looks totally dumb."

"Wes!" Cole said as his daughter's face crumpled.

"Well, they do!" Wes said with another glare at Bree before tromping down the hall to his room. But Bree had already turned Brooke back to the mirror, her hands on her shoulders.

"Tell me something," she said calmly, her face close to Brooke's. "Is anything different now than it was before your brother came home?"

After a moment, the girl shook her head.

"Then what's real? What he said? Or what you see? How you *feel*?"

"I guess…what I feel?"

"Right answer. And brothers suck at seeing their sisters as actual human beings. Believe me, I know. I lived through three of 'em. At some point, we all have to learn how to go with what makes us happy." She gently fingered the girl's hair off her shoulder. "With what makes *you* happy. Because looking to anyone else for approval is an exercise in futility." In the mirror, Cole saw Bree's gaze shift to his, clearly seeking backup.

"She's right, honey. You look amazing. No matter what your brother—or anyone else—thinks."

After a moment, Brooke swung around to give Sabrina a hug, then looked back at Cole. "You still want to see the rest of the stuff?"

"Of course."

"I should go, though," Bree said after the girl went back down the hall.

"You don't—"

"Yeah. I do. What just happened…it had nothing to do with Brooke and everything to do with Wes being uncomfortable with my being here."

Cole frowned. "Except he knows—"

"What he knows," she said gently, "is that grown-ups can't always be trusted. And that, as far as he's concerned…" Her gaze drifted down the hall for a moment before returning to touch Cole's. "I've already broken my promise, by interfering. So…" She gathered up her purse from beside the front door. "I'll get out of your hair."

Except he didn't want her to leave. Which was nuts, because she was right about Wes and because the timing sucked and because life was a helluva lot more complicated than even the most complex video game. And nobody knew better than him that things didn't work out simply because you wanted them to. Human will only went so far. Or, in his case, nowhere.

But to see that smile on his daughter's face…

When he stepped around Bree to open the front door, she looked up, her eyes slightly wide. Startled. Cole smiled. Keeping it light. Cool.

"Well. Thanks again."

"My pleasure," she said, then hesitated a moment too long before finally going outside, her ponytail bobbing as she returned to her car.

"Where's Sabrina?" Brooke said behind him as he pushed the door shut.

"She left," Cole said, turning to see his daughter in another pair of jeans and a light blue top with glittery stuff on it, worn over a longer, darker blue top.

"Stupid Wes," the girl muttered, and Cole was tempted to agree with her.

Except, truthfully? Right now his son was probably the only thing keeping Cole from repeating history. A blessing, really.

Even if in a really crappy disguise.

Chapter Six

It was nearly nine by the time Sabrina got back to her father's house, where she found Pop in the sunroom overlooking the backyard—her mother's favorite spot during her last months, and where he seemed to spend a lot of time. And now, holding a one-way conversation with someone who wasn't there.

Except to him.

"You would've gotten such a kick out of it, Jeannie," Pop said softly, rocking in his favorite chair. Now Sabrina saw he was holding the framed five-by-seven of Mom that usually sat on a small wicker table, facing the garden. "After all the grief Tyler put us through, it did my heart good, to see him so happy. So settled. That Laurel, she's turned him right around. And you'd love her little boy. Their little boy now. Smiles and laughs all the time…"

The rocker creaked when he leaned forward to set the picture back. "And Matt's new baby—he and Kelly named her after you. His birth mother, too. Or did I already tell

you that? Funny, how you always said they'd end up together." He softly chuckled. "I thought you were off your
nut, even thinking such a thing. Told you so, too, as I recall. But you were right, sweetheart. Same as you were
about most things."

Folding his arms across his stomach, he leaned back in
the chair. "So that's three of 'em settled, now that Ethan's
found someone to make him happy again. The kids are all
crazy about Claire. You'd be, too. She's nothing like Merri,
but that's okay. She's exactly what he needs—what they all
need—and that's what matters, right?"

Then he sighed. "Don't really know what's up with
Abby, she never says very much. She's young yet, though.
So no hurry there. Our little Sabrina, though—"

Her stomach jumped.

"If you've got a moment," her father went on, "you might
want to mention her to the Big Guy, 'cause she's having
a hard time of it right now. Only if it seems appropriate,
though—I'm not sure what the protocol is for these things,
if I can go straight to Him or I have to go through chan-
nels. So you do whatever feels best."

He leaned forward again to touch Jeanne's picture, but
now his voice was too low for Sabrina to make out whatever
he was saying. Silently, she slipped back into the kitchen,
taking a moment to steady her thudding heart. Bad enough
she was already shaky after what had happened at Cole's,
her chest caving at that soft look he'd given his daughter…
then cramping at Wes's harsh, mistrustful one.

The one that kept her from drifting off to fantasyland.

Blinking, Sabrina opened, then slammed shut, the fridge
so Pop would know she was home.

"That you, Sabrina?"

"Yep. Want a soda?"

"Sure. A ginger ale, if there is one."

A minute later, she handed him his drink, then popped
the tab to her diet cola before sinking onto the cushioned

love seat a few feet from his chair. The Colonel opened his own can, taking a long swallow before glancing in her direction.

"So how'd it go?"

"Good." She glanced down at the soda, realized she didn't want it. "It's crazy, though, how his parents' house looks exactly the same. Talk about a blast from the past. Cole even said he repainted it the same colors, a couple of summers ago."

"*He* repainted it?"

"Yep. Man of many talents, that one. Anyway, then Cole's sister Diana appeared, she ended up going shopping with Brooke and me. It was…fun."

Pop gave her a shrewd look. "Did it take your mind off things?"

"Enough." *Only to fill it with even more junk to deal with. Yay.*

After a moment, Pop said, "I know what I said, the other night. And I'm not going to say I'm not relieved. That doesn't mean it doesn't gut me, seeing you go through this. Seeing your heart broken."

Sabrina finally took a sip of her soda, a little startled to realize how little she'd thought about Chad and that whole mess all afternoon. Hmm. "More bruised, I think. Not broken."

"You sure?"

"Obviously I'm disappointed. It hurts—a lot—that something I thought was working, wasn't. Didn't. But the longer I'm here, the more I realize I'm not nearly as devastated as I thought I'd be. As I should be."

"That wouldn't be you *admitting* I was right, would it?"

"May…be," she said, and he softly laughed, then rubbed his palm across his khakied knee before his expression turned more serious.

"Don't think there's a parent in the world who wouldn't like to wave a magic wand when one of their kids is in pain, make it all better. Even though that's how we grow. Get stronger." He lifted the can to her in a mock toast. "So here's to better days ahead, kiddo. For all of us."

She leaned forward to gently clink her can against his. "Here's to," she said, and her dad nodded. And damned if her eyes didn't flood again as she realized how much she loved this man. Yes, even when he annoyed the hell out of her.

"And how's Cole doing?" he asked. "With the kids?"

"Coping," she said. Because adding "brilliantly" would probably have come across as overkill. And not exactly objective.

"They seem like good kids."

"They are. From what I've witnessed." *Even if Wes sees me as a jagged-toothed, fiery-eyed monster.*

"Still can't wrap my head around that kid having kids of his own."

"I know, right?"

Pop smiled, then said, "Always liked that boy. Oh, sure, he was a little quiet, maybe. But a good head on his shoulders. Grounded. And he was always respectful. Which was more than I could say about some of those turkeys you brought home."

Then he gave her a pointed look, and she sighed. "Pop—"

"And he worshipped you. Yes, he did," he said when Sabrina's mouth fell open. "I know, I know—that was then and this is now—"

"And *now* women don't want to be worshipped. Or at least I sure don't."

"Says the gal who's had how many relationships go belly-up?"

"Really, Pop?"

"Sorry. Okay, I'm not. Because it's true. Oh, don't give me that look—I'm not saying women are intellectually less than men, or delicate little flowers that need a man's protection. I would hope you know me better than that. That you'd remember what I drummed into your brothers' heads. Hell, what I admired most about your mother was her strength. Her intelligence. Woman put me to shame on both counts more times than I can count. Which is *why*..."

His gaze drifted back toward Jeanne's picture. "I worshipped her. *Cherished* her." Then to Sabrina, he said, "Which is what a man does—or should, anyway—when he's lucky enough to find a woman willing to put up with him. And you know something else? *You deserve nothing less.* So think on that for a minute, missy."

As she sat there, stunned, the Colonel pushed himself to his feet, carrying his can over to the open French door, the damp night air still shimmering with the day's warmth.

"I've been giving a lot of thought to what you said, the other night." His eyes met hers. "About the house."

The conversational right turn brought more than a little trickle of relief. The for-sale sign had disappeared a couple days before the wedding, actually. When she'd asked about it, however, Pop only said he'd taken it off the market until he decided what he wanted to do. That he'd gotten his deposit back from Sunridge, although two units would be available in the next couple of months, if he changed his mind.

"And?"

He pressed his lips together. "You know, ever since our conversation, I could practically hear your mother reading me the riot act for acting like some wishy-washy ninny. For being scared of *moving*, for God's sake. Really, how crazy is that?"

Sabrina smiled. "Pretty crazy. So...you've decided to...?"

Honestly, she felt like a reality TV host, waiting for his answer.

"Sell. And, yes, I'm sure this time. But the Realtor's right. The place needs help. Painting, what she called 'staging.'" He made air quotes. "So it doesn't look like a set from *Leave It to Beaver*?"

"More like *That '70s Show*. But, yeah."

"So will you help?"

"Me? I dress people, not houses."

"So think of the house like a person. And the agent said she's got a list of places that rent furniture and—" he waved one hand "—all the little stuff."

"Accessories?"

"Whatever. Although first we've got to clear out all this junk, get the house painted. If I can find someone who doesn't charge an arm and a leg. For slapping paint on some walls, for God's sake. But unfortunately since you guys have the temerity to have lives of your own, I may not have any other choice—"

Sabrina clamped her mouth shut to keep in the laugh. "Some" walls? The house was nearly 3,500 square feet. That was a lot of walls—

"Although maybe Cole and the kids would like to help?"

Wait. What?

"What?"

"You just said he repainted his parents' house. And you think I don't remember him painting your room? That hideous pink… There's a reason I never go in there." He shuddered. "But the point is, he knows how. And when he was here the other day he sounded like he was looking for things for the kids to do."

"I somehow doubt painting your house was what he had in mind. Or the kids."

"Won't know until you ask him."

"*I* ask him?"

"You took his daughter shopping. He owes you one. Right?"

"I think your logic is a little skewed there—"

"Saturday would be good," Pop said, getting to his feet. "I can probably strong-arm your brother into helping, at least for part of the day. Between Cole and Matt, and you, and the kids, I figure we could probably knock out at least the downstairs pretty quickly. Because I'd like to get the house back on the market as soon as possible."

Then, clearly considering this to be a "he spake, and it was done" deal, he walked away.

Brother.

Fortunately—or unfortunately, depending on how you looked at it—she already had Cole's number in her phone. When he picked up, however, she immediately said, "You don't have to say yes…"

It was true, nobody had twisted his arm, Cole thought on Saturday when he and the kids arrived at Preston's. But it was also true that the kids were already going stir-crazy—they'd enrolled in a couple of summer programs, yeah, but those weren't starting until July. And it wasn't as though he'd ever forget how good the Nobles had been to him, how generous Jeanne had been with her affection. The Colonel, too, in his own way. How he made every kid who'd ever spent more than five minutes in his presence feel important. As if he or she had a purpose, even if that purpose hadn't yet fully made itself known. A real shot in the arm for a kid who'd spent most of his childhood feeling like an outcast.

So that's why he was here. Not for Bree, and not for himself, but for the man who'd seen the *more* in Cole long before he had.

"Hey, guys," Matt said with a grin for the kids when he opened the door. "Sabrina brought doughnuts, they're in the kitchen. Go help yourselves."

"What kind?" Brooke asked, frowning slightly.

Amusement danced in Matt's dark eyes. "Does it matter?"

"I don't like those jelly ones."

"Neither does my sister. So you're golden."

Then both kids looked at Cole. "Dad?" Wes asked.

"I think you'll burn it off. Go for it," he said, and they did. Literally. Before he could change his mind.

"One thing Erin and I agreed on," he said when Matt frowned at him, "was that we'd limit their sweets. So this is a treat."

"Gotcha," Matt said, leading Cole into the living room, nearly empty save for a few pieces of furniture shoved to the center of the dusty, marred wood floor, the old damask draperies huddled in one corner. "Kelly sent casseroles, too. Since after she got up with the baby at whatever ungodly hour, she apparently got inspired to cook. Woman's bat-crap crazy," he said with a smile that said that was fine with him.

"Thanks, but I'm good." Not really hungry—and not awake enough yet to face the woman who'd regularly invaded his thoughts and dreams way too often the past week—Cole glanced around the room. "Wow. This is... strange."

"Gonna be even more strange after we paint and Bree does her thing with the place. Still mostly neutrals on the walls, but some of the stuff she's stashed in the garage..." Shaking his head, Matt took a screwdriver to a set of ancient miniblinds over the window. "Apparently she kept running things by Kelly—you haven't seen our house yet, but 'subtle' is not a word I'd use to describe my wife's decorating style—" Amazing, how much love could be packed into two little words. *My wife.* "—and between the two of them..." He released an exaggerated sigh. "There will be color. And...sparkle."

Cole chuckled. "Where's your gang?"

"The kids, you mean? The older two spent the night with their grandmother. Their dad's mom." He grinned. "And the baby's a little young to be put to work just yet."

"And your dad?"

"Out for his usual morning walk. Because God forbid he alter his routine." The newly freed blinds clattered to the floor, flooding the room with early morning light through the now-bare window. Matt bent to gather the blinds, strangling them with their own cord.

"If you don't wanna eat, grab that roll of painter's tape and let's get the room prepped. Gotta leave at two—it's my day to work with the kids over at All Saints—which is why we needed to start so early. Sorry."

Cole started taping around the hundred-year-old marble fireplace that had survived God knew how many children over the years before he asked, "Work with the kids?"

"What? Oh. Yeah. One of the priests there is this young guy—well, like our age, that's young, right? Anyway, dude got the youth group up and running again for the first time in years. Kids from all over Maple River, all backgrounds. It's in the church, but it's not about the church, if you know what I mean. If the kids want to talk about religion, that's fine, but things tend to stay pretty ecumenical."

"Sounds cool."

"What it is is one of the most positive things I've seen happen in this town, *to* this town, in years. In any case, word got out that Father Bill needed adults to help. You know, teaching classes or coming in and shooting some hoops, whatever. Not a whole lot to do around here, as I'm sure you remember. Especially for those kids whose parents maybe can't shell out the bucks to let them do organized sports. Or who aren't interested. Of course, you never know who's going to show up. Some days, nobody. Other days, I swear it's like half of Jersey is there." Matt swiped a wet sponge across the grungy windowsill, tossed it into a sudsy bucket. "Gets *really* loud."

"I can imagine—"

"There you are," Bree said, appearing like a genie in the wide archway separating the living and dining rooms. She was wearing a pair of those oddball pants that couldn't seem to make a commitment whether to be long or short, and what Cole guessed was one of her father's old shirts.

And yet, with her hair loosely pinned up so that half of it feathered around her face, she still looked hot. Even with the dark circles under her eyes that told of a sleepless night. "What? You can't come say hello? Eat my doughnuts? I bought enough to feed the block."

"No. Thanks," Cole said, and he saw understanding bloom in her eyes. Along with embarrassment, maybe.

"Coffee, then?" she said gently. From the back of the house, he heard his kids laughing. And another laugh he couldn't place. So he and Bree wouldn't be alone. Good.

"Sure."

"Then, follow me."

However, on the way she ducked into the sunroom to retrieve an abandoned glass, only to be then diverted by a robin splashing in a stone birdbath a few feet out in the yard. Cole stood in the doorway, his hands in his pockets as he watched her, aching for her sadness and wondering why there weren't cheat codes for relationships. A list of shortcuts to help you avoid the bombs and the traps and the monsters waiting to knock you on your ass.

Or send you back to Level 1.

Sucking in a breath, Cole scanned the glowing room. "Didn't this used to be a porch?"

"Pop fixed it up for Mom," Bree said, scooping a crumpled napkin off the sisal rug, a plate from the coffee table. "When she got sick."

"Your mom was great." He paused. "But then, your dad's not exactly shabby, either."

"Says the person who didn't have to live with him," Bree said on sort of a laughed sigh. "Don't get me wrong, I love the old guy. Always have. Most generous man on the fricking planet. But some of us had a harder time dealing with his parenting style than others. Or rather, he had a harder time dealing with our personalities. Like Tyler's." Her mouth pulled to one side. "And mine."

Cole grinned. "You have to admit, you were a bit like a

jack-in-the-box. Poor guy probably never knew when you were going to go all *blah!* in his face."

"Heh. That's one way of putting it."

"And now?"

"We've both mellowed, I think. He seems to have, anyway. And I've gotten better at controlling the explosions. At least, I'm no longer my hormones' bitch. I might feel the dramatics bubbling inside me, but I don't indulge them as often. And God, I'm sorry…" Balancing the dishes against her middle, she started out of the sunroom. "Didn't mean to…whatever this was."

"Have a conversation?"

Her mouth thinned. "Revert to old patterns."

"And maybe some of those patterns weren't so bad. Once upon a time, we were good. Good friends, I mean," he added when her eyebrows lifted. "Maybe you don't think we can go there again, but I don't see why not."

And, yes, that was the sound of his earlier resolve crumbling like dry sand. Because back before things went south between them, he'd never felt her equal, never felt he had any way of paying her back for everything she'd done for him. *That* had been the real Bree. As was this one, a woman whose love for her family—even her father, he thought with a slight smile—shimmered through her words. And then there was her affection for his daughter, natural and unfeigned, born out of who she simply was. That other Bree had been an aberration. A phantom. An illusion.

But the one standing here now needed him to return a long-overdue favor. Whether she knew it or not.

"And maybe I don't see why you'd want to," she said.

Taken by themselves, her words might have sounded like a slap in the face. Except from the wretched look on hers, Cole guessed they were directed far more at herself than him. And it killed him, to hear what almost sounded like defeat in her voice. Killed him more to not wrap his arms around her. Simply to hold her. Not like back then, when he'd been a startled, horny, fumbling mess, but like he wanted to now. Like he *could* now.

However, all he did was shrug, as if it was no big deal. "Maybe because I'm curious to see if our upgraded software makes the interface run any more smoothly."

At that, she snuffled a laugh. "And what does it say about me, that I actually got that? Except…I'm not going to stick around, you know."

"So you said."

"And I can't—"

"Friends, Bree. That's all."

"Okay," she breathed out, before finally heading for the kitchen.

Which, even on the second viewing, was a shock, the gleaming space refusing to jibe with his memory of it. Scarfing down doughnuts and orange juice, the kids were seated at the granite island across from a ponytailed blonde who looked barely older than Brooke, although Cole knew she had to be in her midtwenties.

Abby grinned. "You ever feed these two?" she said in a low, scratchy voice as Sabrina sidled up to Brooke and snitched a piece of the kid's chocolate-glazed doughnut, earning her an indignant, but good-natured, squeal…and a glower from Wes.

"Only on Tuesdays and alternate Saturdays," Cole said, deadpan, ignoring the glower, and Brooke's mouth sagged open.

"Dad. Really?"

Cole chuckled. "I take it you're on the painting crew?" he said to Abby as Bree handed him a mug of steaming coffee.

"Only part-time." The blonde clutched her own coffee to her chest before glancing at her sister. "I assume those guys told you about Tyler and me having this salvage business?" When Cole nodded, she grinned. "Those cousins from HGTV are over there filming today. They're using the place as a resource for a house they're redoing nearby. Otherwise Ty'd be here, too. He says the place is crawling with camera dudes and producers and such."

"That's awesome. But you didn't want to be on TV?"

"Me? No way—"

"So anybody gonna help me out here, or what?" Matt called from the living room, and for a moment Cole warped back to his adolescence, the warmth and laughter and good-natured ribbing that had always been part of the Noble household. Despite knowing the reprise was only tempo-rary, it felt good, being back. Damn good.

Never mind his son's death glares every time Cole even looked at Bree, or every time Brooke laughed at something she said. Or that—her cautious surrender to the idea of their being friends again notwithstanding—it was obvious that what was broken between them was still beyond any real repair. And probably always would be. Even if they patched things up, they'd always be able to see the scar.

And he already had enough of those, thank you.

As did his kids. Which he'd do well to remember.

Stretching out her lower back, Sabrina surveyed her handiwork—four walls in a sagey green the agent had ap-parently sworn to Pop was the "in" color for living spaces these days. Whatever. By the time the floors were refin-ished and she added those hot-pink-and-coral throw pil-lows to the safe beige sofa Mom had bought the year before she died, maybe nobody would notice the color made ev-eryone's skin tone look as if they'd tangled with some bad sushi.

Pop would periodically stick his head in and frown—although at the booming rock music from Matt's docked iPhone or the paint color, Sabrina wasn't sure. But she guessed the only way he'd get through this was to pretend it was happening to someone else's house.

At least the morning had passed quickly, with two

freshly painted rooms to show for it—Matt and Sabrina and Brooke tackling the living room, while Cole, Wes and Abby polished off the adjacent dining room. Probably a blessing the music had prevented any real conversation, even if the pounding beat had done nothing to quiet Sabrina's overactive brain.

Because the disapproving looks Wes aimed in her direction whenever she and Brooke got to laughing about something nearly killed her. At first she'd chalked up his grumpiness to being a thirteen-year-old boy who'd been dragged out of bed too early, but she finally couldn't deny that, nope, it was her.

Still.

And again.

"And that's a wrap," her brother said, hammering the lid back on the last paint can. "You guys 'bout done in there?" he called over to the others, finishing up in what looked like a permanent pool of sunshine from the dining room's custard-colored walls.

"Pretty much," Cole called back, and despite her muddled mental state, Sabrina had to smile—there was nearly as much paint on him and Wes as the walls. Then his gaze snagged in hers, and she remembered why she'd frankly been grateful they'd ended up on different "crews" this morning. Because that chitchat earlier? The patience and understanding in those soft gray eyes? Honest to God, she'd practically had to hang on to something to keep from being sucked into his gravitational pull. Because all she wanted, right then, was to feel those now-solid arms around her, to wrap her own arms around his waist and hold on tight.

And that would be bad, bad, bad. For so, so, *so* many reasons. Two of whom were now trying to attack each other with paint-soaked rollers.

"Guys, honestly," Cole said wearily over his daughter's shrieks, and Sabrina smiled.

Because this really wasn't about attraction—

Yeah, right, she thought, watching him stretch to paint the dining room's window trim, the soft cotton of his T-shirt clinging to actual muscles. Between their history and his hotness and her horniness, her hormones were downright salivating. Kids or no kids. But much, much more than that, it was about this aura Cole had always had about him, making her feel safe. That no matter what, she could trust him.

And *safe* was about the most *un*safe thing she could feel right now. Because who she didn't dare trust was herself—

"Hey," Matt said beside her, making her jump. "Have you heard a word I said?"

"What? Oh. No. Sorry."

Her brother shook his head. "I was saying, you should go with me to All Saints. Meet the kids." When she frowned, he said, "The girls, they'd be beside themselves getting to talk to somebody in fashion. Some of 'em might even be up for a makeover. Like Cole said you did for Brooke?"

"Oh. Uh…"

"Look," he said, lowering his voice, "there's a few who could maybe stand to tone it down a little in the makeup and show-everything-you-got department. I'm talking thir-teen-, fourteen-year-old girls trying to look like they're twenty-five. Not to mention act like it."

She laughed. "Honey, Jersey girls are born flamboyant. I think it's something in the water—"

"This goes beyond that. A lot of the girls come with their brothers—their older brothers—and I can tell they're look-ing to hook up. And before you get on my case, I don't think that dressing sexy necessarily means a girl—or woman—is 'asking' for it. Or that a guy has the right to assume she is. Which is part of what I talk about with the boys, about self-control and respect and boundaries." He smirked. "Until they're probably sick of hearing me run my mouth. Same stuff Pop drummed into our heads when we were kids."

"Heh. I got the same spiel, you know. From Mom, but whatever."

"Except not all of these kids are lucky enough to get those spiels. And the problem is, some of these girls *are* asking for…whatever they think dressing like that will get them. Because they think that's all they've got. All they are."

Sabrina looked out the window toward the front yard as her brother continued. "And it's been bugging me for some time," he said, "how to handle it. Father Bill, too. Father Bill, *especially*. Not exactly what he had in mind when he started the program up again. I mean, nothing happens at the center, but outside of it…I don't know. And it seems to me you're someone they could relate to. Because you're young and cool and you always look good. To me, anyway."

Blowing a laugh through her nose, she faced him again. *"Young?"*

"Compared to the old ladies who stop by to deliver cookies and juice? Definitely. And you obviously get on good with kids. Seriously, Brooke hardly left your side the whole morning. So, please? Just go talk to them, okay?" Matt said, giving her shoulder a squeeze before he walked away, his request churning in her head.

Not to mention her stomach.

Because, she thought as she watched Cole gather up his painting gear, she'd been such an exemplary teenager herself, right?

Chapter Seven

Having already cleaned his own brushes and rollers outside, Cole followed the sound of running water to find Bree washing her hands at the kitchen's oversize stainless steel sink, frowning at something outside the window. His paint-spattered kids, he saw when he came up behind her, both sprawled on a pair of chairs on the deck as if they'd just finished running a marathon.

Bree jumped. "Cripes…give a person a heads-up."

"Sorry." He ripped a paper towel off the nearby standing holder and handed it to her. Her mouth pressed tight, she roughly scrubbed the towel over her hands, slam-dunked it into the trash. "Hey. You okay?"

Her arms crossed, she stared back out the window. "Matt asked me to help out at the center."

"Yeah? Me, too."

"He suggested you give the girls makeovers?"

He softly laughed, even as he wondered why her brother's request had so obviously upset her. "No," he said, leaning back against the counter with his fingers in his pockets. "Computer tips. I pointed out, however, they probably all navigate the web better than I do. Diana's brats were computer savvy by three. Crazy."

Still not looking at him, she said, "So you said no?"

"Actually, it might be a another way for Wes and Brooke to meet other kids their age. So I said I'd think about it."

When she didn't respond, Cole went to the fridge and pulled out a bottle of water. Same as he used to, when this kitchen had been like Penn Station. Even if that old fridge could have fit inside this one. Twisting off the cap, he looked back at Bree, his forehead cramping at her almost-tormented expression as she kept looking out the damn window.

"Bree? What's wrong?"

"Nothing—"

"Friends, remember? So give it up, dude."

At that, she smiled, but a long moment passed before she said, "What Matt was saying, about the girls...it brought back a lot of not-so-good memories. Of me at that age. God, I was so messed up."

"Who among us wasn't?"

"Yeah, but Matt has no idea *how* messed up I was." She paused. "What it led to."

Memories stirred, of previous conversations. Conversations his pathetic, lonely, younger self had endured only because he couldn't think of any other way to keep the connection. Except, again, the quietly conflicted woman in front of him didn't even seem related to that histrionic teenage girl who'd seemed determined to blame everyone else for her problems. Had that been the case, the new improved Cole would have handed her a tissue, patted her on the back, said, "Laters," and walked away.

But it wasn't. And he couldn't.

"And I thought we'd moved past that—"

"For God's sake, Cole—who am I to talk to some girl

about self-esteem issues? About how she needs to respect herself?"

His forehead knotted. "And where's this coming from? Seriously, how's helping out those girls any different than what you did with Brooke? Did *for* her?"

"Because your daughter's nothing like I was." A sad smile curved her mouth. "I could fake it with her. From what Matt said, I'm guessing those girls…" Her head wagged. "They'd see straight through me, know I was a fraud."

"Yeah, I could really tell how much you were *pretending* with Brooke. And like you could fake anything with anybody. So I call BS. And why are you being so hard on yourself?"

"Not hard. Honest."

"Hey. Look at me." When she did, he said, "Everybody does stupid stuff when they're young. You're not some special snowflake, okay?" That got a tiny smile. "And besides, you weren't the one who walked away."

"Which you wouldn't have done if I hadn't gone nuts on you."

"Okay, valid point," he said, and she snorted. "Still doesn't make either of us bad people. Temporarily insane, maybe. But not bad—"

"I know I'm not bad, Cole," she said, sounding tired. "At least, not anymore—"

"Dammit, Bree—you're human. And humans screw up. Own it, already."

At that, she finally cracked a real smile…only to immediately blow out a breath. "If it were only that easy."

Setting the bottle on the counter, Cole leaned back against it again, his arms folded as he frowned down at the floor. "What's easy," he said, "is hiding. Coddling your fears, refusing to face what scares you." He lifted his eyes to hers. "Only, where does that get you? Nowhere, that's where. Fear…it's paralyzing. Believe me, I know. What I finally realized, though, is that unless we stare that sucker down, act in spite of it instead of because of it…it wins, doesn't it?"

"Wow," she said softly, then angled her head, her brows drawn. "So…you're not afraid anymore?"

"You kidding? Now that I've got the kids full-time?" He shook his head. "It's an ongoing struggle, believe me. But the moment I held Wes right after he was born, it hit me—over the sheer terror—that I had no choice but to be who this kid needed his father to be." One side of his mouth tucked up. "And that sure as hell wasn't who I'd always believed I was."

Outside, some bird sang its heart out while their gazes tangled, until, finally, Bree released a breath. "I do hear what you're saying, but…I'm not there yet."

"Again, BS. Because who do you think planted that seed to begin with? Yeah," he said when her eyes shot to his, "chew on that for a minute."

After rapping on the kitchen window to motion to the kids to meet him out front, he briefly met Bree's still stunned gaze, then headed for the door. Before he could open it, however, the floor creaked behind him.

"Thanks," Bree said when he turned.

"For…?"

"Being a friend?"

"Always," he said softly, then started to let himself out the door. Only to look back and say, "And you know what else? If your experiences could benefit even one of those girls, keep her from going down a path she's going to regret, who are you to withhold that from her?"

And if she never spoke to him again, it was tempting to think her shocked expression had been totally worth it.

His words had rocked her.

Not so much the words themselves, though, as the man saying the words, Sabrina thought as, two hours later, she continued sorting the junk in her old room into pitch, keep and donate boxes—although the keep box was definitely the least filled of the three.

Funny how she'd always thought of herself as the stronger of the two in the relationship…until that embarrassing episode in the backseat of his parents' Honda Civic, when she'd shown her hand—and pretty much everything else. At that moment, her fragile facade had crumbled, even if she hadn't realized until then that her all-that-ness had been a facade. That everything she'd thought she'd known about herself had been a lie.

And now, everything she'd thought she'd known about Cole.

Slamming a decrepit doll that should have been tossed years ago into the garbage box, tears burned behind her eyes—

"Bree?" Kelly called from downstairs. "You around?"

Damn. She'd forgotten that everybody in the whole frickin' family had a key. Swiping her cheeks, Sabrina shoved to her feet and tromped out onto the landing.

"Up here. Packing."

Seconds later, her old friend started up the stairs, little Teri clutched to her chest. "I can't get over how different the place looks already," she said breathlessly when she reached the top. "I take it the Colonel's not here?"

"Nope. He's over at Sunridge, checking out his new digs. Deciding what to take, I imagine." Sabrina reached for the sleeping infant, whom Kelly hesitantly relinquished. Then the redhead turned, softly gasping at the stairwell's wall, the dingy white paint ghosted with dozens of blank rectangles. "It looks so…naked. What's happening with all the pictures?"

"Some will go with Pop, I imagine. Yes, they will, won't they, sweetie?" she said, gently bouncing her tiny, frowning niece. "And I guess we'll divvy up the rest." Her gaze swung to Kelly. "And to what do I owe the honor?"

Her friend snorted. "Cabin fever. Kids are still with their grandmother, and I realized if I didn't get out of the house I'd go bonkers. So baby-pie and I walked over. Well, I walked, she strollered."

"And of all the places you could have gone, you chose here?"

Her cheeks pinking, Kelly shoved a tangle of curls behind her ear. "Matt said he invited you to go to the center. And that you seemed less than enthusiastic—"

"Hey, want something to drink?" Sabrina asked, starting down the stairs with the baby. "There's some fancy-schmancy bottled tea—"

"And you seriously think tea's gonna throw me off the scent?"

Near the bottom of the stairs, Sabrina spun around, making Kelly practically snatch her cooing daughter from Sabrina's arms. Folding those arms over the resulting emptiness, Sabrina said, "You know, I think I liked you better when you were all mousy and stuff."

"Sorry, cookie, that ship has sailed. Thank God. And I didn't shove the stroller over every damn tree root between my house and this one to be put off. I have diapers. And an unlimited supply of breast milk. So I'm not leaving until you tell me what's up with you."

Clearly, not an empty threat.

Two bottles of tea later, Kelly sat cross-legged on the old family room sofa, her daughter at her breast, frowning at Sabrina. Who'd told her everything.

As in, *every*thing.

"Wow. I can't…" Her friend blinked. "Wow."

Curled up on the recliner, Sabrina's mouth pulled tight. "Yep. And it was every bit as awkward and regrettable as you're imagining."

"Uh, no. Some places, I refuse to go. But…" Her brows pushed together, Kelly slightly tilted her head. "Really?

Not that you did it—although color me gobsmacked—but that you're still beating yourself up over it?"

"You weren't around back then. I wasn't a very nice person. To Cole, especially. No wonder he ditched me. Hell, *I* would have ditched me."

"And you were both kids who had no idea how to handle what had happened," Kelly said gently.

"We were seventeen, Kell. Old enough." Sabrina let her head loll back onto the smooth, soft leather. "The funny thing is, it's not like I've spent the past however many years doing the mea culpa thing about what happened. But between coming back here—and *why* I'm back—and seeing Cole again, and then Matt asking me to help those girls…I dunno. A lot of old junk bubbling to the surface, I guess."

Kelly frowned at her for a moment, then propped little Teri on her lap, rubbing her back until she let out a loud belch. "Honestly, you are so your daddy's child," she murmured, then laid the infant on the couch, where she promptly yawned and passed out, her wispy red hair quivering in the ceiling fan's gentle breeze, and Sabrina thought *she'd* pass out from the sweetness.

"So now you're feeling sorry for yourself."

Sabrina's brows pushed together. "For acting like an ass? Hardly. Mad at myself, though? You bet."

"Then you need to get over it. Because there is no 'fixing' the past. We can learn from it, maybe, but lugging all those old regrets around with us is simply dumb. And what Cole said about handling your fears…he's right. The only way to ditch those suckers is to face them head-on. I've been there, honey," she said softly. "Dude speaks the truth."

Smiling slightly, Kelly let her gaze drop again to her daughter, that adorable mouth sucking in her sleep. "It's so, so easy to let the past trip us up. Or to let our mistakes define us. Our…choices." As Kelly toyed with her baby's hand, Sabrina thought about her friend's first marriage, to a man she'd assumed would protect her, care for her. And his children. Didn't work out that way.

As if reading her thoughts, Kelly said, "Sure, I screwed up before, choosing Rick. Staying in my marriage probably far longer than I should have. And I'm not gonna say part of me doesn't still regret that, at least on some level."

Her gaze met Sabrina's again. "But that doesn't mean I don't think I deserve what I have now, with your brother. And frankly, if I hadn't made those mistakes? I don't think I would appreciate him—our life—half as much as I do. Also, if I were in your position, having the chance to share with kids at the center what I know now? You bet your butt I'd take it."

"And what makes you think they'd listen?"

"Why do you assume they wouldn't?"

"Because if they're like me at that age—"

"And what if they are? Seems to me that would only make you relate to them even better, right?"

Her words were close enough to Cole's to make Sabrina flinch. As well as realize that wallowing in guilt wasn't gonna cut it.

A long, harsh breath left her lungs.

"How long does this thing at the church go on?"

Grinning, her friend gave her a thumbs-up.

Over the squeaks of a dozen kids' sneakers as they shot hoops on the worn church hall floor, the loud *clang!* of the metal door opening made Wesley look over…and his stomach dropped. Although, truthfully? Dad's friend looked as unsure about being there as Wes felt, her hands in her back pockets and her face pinched. Then his stomach twisted again when his sister jumped up from beside their dad to give Sabrina a hug—

"Wes!" Matt called out, blowing his whistle. "Look sharp!"

His head swung around a second before the ball bounced

in front of him; Wes easily intercepted it, dribbling it down the court and slam-dunking it through the hoop. It wasn't a real game, they were only fooling around and stuff, but Wesley felt his face warm at the smattering of applause. He wasn't good at a lot of sports—and didn't care—but basketball was okay. And Dad had already said, when they found their house, if there wasn't a hoop they could get one.

A thought that made him look back toward the bleachers, where Sabrina was talking to Dad and his sister, both of them looking at Sabrina like she had them hypnotized or something.

Breathing hard, Wes stalked off the court to a refreshment table set up at the back of the hall. Nothing fancy—the cookies looked gross—but at least there was a cooler with bottled water and juice. He'd just twisted off the cap of a bottle of grape juice when some grinning black dude in baggy green basketball shorts, maybe a year or two older than Wes, came up to him.

"Impressive," he said, giving Wes a fist bump.

"What? Oh. Thanks."

The kid stuck out his hand. "Elijah Hawkins."

"Wesley. Wes. Rayburn."

"You new?"

"Um…kind of. I mean, my grandparents live here, so my dad and sister and I are hanging out for the summer, house-sitting."

"So you're not sticking around?"

"I'm not sure. Maybe?" He shrugged.

"Well, if you are? I'm on the team over at Hoover, we could really use you."

"Hoover—that's the high school, right? Sorry—I'm only thirteen."

"Get out. Really? Tall as you are, I would've thought you were at least fifteen, maybe even sixteen. Well, look— my friends and I, we get up a game over here most nights, around seven or so. You're welcome to join us anytime, okay?"

"Uh, sure. Thanks."

With a wave, the guy loped back out on to the court, and Wes sighed. Wasn't worth telling him they didn't live close enough to the church for him to come over whenever he felt like it. Or that he'd probably be going to a private school. Which always sounded a little snotty, frankly.

But right then, he thought as his gaze drifted back to the bleachers, he had far more important things to worry about. Anxiety spearing through him, he dumped his empty bottle in the recycling bin and ran back out onto the court, hoping maybe if he kept moving, he wouldn't think.

"So, no girls here today?" Sabrina asked, sitting on the other side of Brooke with her hands tightly laced over one knee. And don't think Cole hadn't caught the *What the hell am I doing here?* look in her eyes—pretty much identical to the one in his daughter's. In fact, the first time the child had unplastered herself from his side had been to hug Bree. Who, he noticed, had traded out her father's shirt for a bright purple top that bared her arms and grazed her hips. And tight jeans which showed off those hips to perfection.

And he could smell her perfume, slicing through the sweet tang of early summer air…mixed with the far less pleasant scent of sweaty teenage boys.

"The girls are upstairs," he said, and Sabrina looked at Brooke, who was wearing one of the new tops Bree had helped her pick out, something frilly and floaty and absolutely perfect for her.

"How come you're not with them?"

"Um…because I don't know them?"

At that, Bree put an arm around the girl's shoulders and gave her a squeeze, then said to Cole over her head, "And how come *you're* not out there playing basketball with the guys?"

"Me? Basketball? Get real."

She chuckled. "Wes seems pretty good at it."

"A trait he definitely did not inherit from me."

Another soft laugh preceded, "So no computer class?"

"Only computer's in the office. Something so old Windows doesn't even support the OS anymore. Clearly your brother hadn't thought that part through—"

A shrill giggle floated down from the catwalk fronting a series of smaller rooms on the upper level, piercing the shouts and grunts from the game. Cole felt Brooke stiffen beside him as Sabrina looked up.

"That them?"

"Yep."

Another wave of giggles floated down. "They sound like fun, don't you think?" she said softly, and Brooke stiffened even more. But it was pretty obvious, when Sabrina raised her eyes again, the battle going on inside her own head. Whatever had goosed her into rethinking things, he knew how much courage it took to break inertia's hold on a battered psyche that only wanted to be left in peace. He was so proud of her he could pop. But he wouldn't tell her that.

Then, as one, and still all yakking at once, the group headed for the stairs. After clumsily clomping down in shoes nearly as big as their heads, they walked toward the snack table set up at the end of the room, showing off an array of baby butts barely contained in short shorts or shrink-wrapped jeans.

Dear God—they'd eat his little girl alive.

"Come on." Getting to her feet, Bree held out her hand to Brooke. "We'll go together."

"Ohmygod, no! I mean, that would look totally lame!"

"Any more lame than sitting over here with us?" she said, and Brooke's gaze shifted to Cole's.

"She's got a point, honey."

"So go on," Sabrina said gently. "Introduce yourself. Bond over the cookies—"

"I already saw them." The kid made a face. "They're, like, totally disgusting."

"Then use that," Cole said. "As an ice breaker."

"A what?"

"A way to get the conversation started."

"Good idea," Bree said. "And what's the worst that can happen?"

"They all look at me like I'm stupid?"

Cole's chest cramped, hearing his old fears in his daughter's words. But before he could figure out how to respond to that, Bree said, "Says the girl brave enough to turn her whole world upside down because the one she was living in wasn't working for her. Somehow, cutie, I don't think you've got anything to worry about."

And there it was, the old Sabrina whose ballsiness used to turn him inside out. Not to mention on. That still did, truth be told. But he wouldn't tell her that, either.

For a long moment, Brooke sat there, watching the girls. Until she suddenly stood, sucked in a breath and headed straight toward them.

Cole leaned over, close enough to get another heady whiff of her perfume, and whispered, "You should give lessons."

Her brow puckered, she looked back at him. "In…?"

"Mojo-finding," he said, and she gave him a smile that zinged straight to The Land That Time Forgot.

And he definitely wouldn't tell her *that.*

Trying to ignore her wobbling knees, Brooke crossed the floor, feeling both Dad's and Sabrina's eyes on her back like a real touch, gently pushing her forward. One of the girls noticed her coming over and poked one of the others. Then they all looked at her, frowning, and for a second she thought about turning and running right back. But she didn't.

"Hey," she said, hoping her voice wasn't shaking as much as her knees. "I'm Brooke."

The girls all mumbled their names—Micaela, Jessica, Caitlin, Shandra. She thought they were all about her age, maybe a little older. It was hard to tell because of how they were dressed. All the makeup and stuff. Brooke picked up a cookie and took a bite, making a face she definitely did not have to fake. One of the girls snickered. Caitlin, she thought. Tons of reddish, curly hair.

"They totally suck, right?"

"This one sure does. Oh, jeez—" Brooke's face flamed. "One of your mothers or grandmothers or somebody didn't bring these, did they?"

"No worries," Caitlin said, her smoky eye makeup so heavy you could hardly see her blue eyes. "But they're free, so, you know." She shrugged.

Another girl, her coloring more like Sabrina's, took one of the cookies, munching on it as she said, "Those your parents over there?"

"What? Oh." She turned. "My dad, yeah. But the woman…she's only a friend."

"*Your* friend? Or your dad's?"

"Well, his, mostly. Like from when they were kids?"

Micaela—that was her name, right—laughed, her long, almost black hair spilling over her shoulders. "Yeah, well, he's sure not looking at her like a *friend*, if you know what I mean."

"And your dad's kind of cute," Jessica said, her green eyes all sparkly. Blonde. Dimples. Really pretty. "For an old guy, I mean."

The others laughed, and Brooke blushed so hard it hurt.

"Hey, you guys," Caitlin said, smacking the girl next to her. "Knock it off. You're embarrassing her. Jeez."

"No, it's okay—"

"Like hell," Caitlin said, and Brooke blushed *again*. "And we're sorry. Aren't we?" she said to the others, who mumbled their apologies. Then Shandra pointed to Brooke's feet. "Where'd you get those shoes? They're, like, supercute."

The others all crowded around as Brooke looked down at her flats, black with little red sparkly stones across the toes. Almost boring compared with all the straps and buckles and stuff on their shoes, but Brooke loved them. "I got them when Sabrina—she's the lady with my dad—took me shopping. Because that's her job, in New York. To help people pick out clothes."

All the girls looked across the floor at Sabrina. Who smiled and waved at them. Caitlin looked back, jamming a hand through her crazy curly hair. "Seriously? That's, like, a real thing?"

"Yeah. She's a personal shopper."

"Huh. She pick out that top, too?"

"The whole outfit, everything."

"So, what?" Jessica said, scowling. Not so pretty now. "You can't choose your own clothes? Like you're a baby?"

For a moment—but only a moment—Brooke felt her eyes sting. Then she thought, *The heck with this,* and said, "She knows all about fashion and style and stuff. I don't. So what's the big deal?"

At that, Caitlin lowered her eyes to her own chest, then back at Brooke. "You think maybe she might help me? Because I have no clue what to do with these," she said, waving a hand over at her breasts. Which were, like, super huge. Seriously.

"Well…" Brooke pretended to think it over, then nodded. "I suppose you could ask…"

Upper East Side matrons, Sabrina could handle, no problem. Dazzle, even. A batch of Jersey adolescents, however…? Never mind she had a lot more in common with them than her Manhattan clients.

But Brooke had barely introduced her to the gang before two of the four—the least outrageously attired of the two, natch—practically attacked her with questions about what she did and where did she get Brooke's clothes and could she help them, too?

"If you like, sure. And everything came from the outlet mall out on the highway," she said, reaching for one of the cookies in a show of solidarity. Thing tasted like sweet dirt, blech. "Because you don't have to spend the big bucks to look good. Something I figured out when I was your age and we had more kids in the house than money. So shopping became a game, you know?"

"Hey, that's what my mom says, too," the one with the biggest hair said. "She's, like, really big into couponing."

"So was mine," Sabrina said, smiling.

"So what's the big deal with clothes, anyway?"

This from Jessica, the blonde. Even more bodaciously curved than Caitlin, amazingly. *Maybe* fourteen. But before Sabrina could answer, Brooke said, "The right ones make you feel good about yourself."

The girl flashed Brooke The Look, then jabbed one hand on her hip. Sabrina guessed there was an older model at home. "I feel plenty good about myself, thank you, exactly the way I am."

"And that's great," Sabrina said, nonchalantly choosing another cookie. "No, really. Because a lot of girls your age—how old are you?"

Chin came up. "Thirteen."

Holy hell. "A lot of thirteen-year-olds hide behind their clothes, partly because they don't really know who they are yet. I sure didn't. But what we put on our bodies says a lot about how we think about ourselves. And how we want other people to see us. Not only as pretty, but as smart. Confident. In charge of our own lives. Not as *things*, but as people."

The girl snorted, but Sabrina could tell her words had struck a chord. A dissonant one, maybe, but a chord nonetheless. But she also knew—because she remembered thirteen like it was last week—that a subject change was definitely in order. And when she took her next bite of the Cookie from Hell, inspiration struck.

"There's a kitchen here, right?"

Shandra frowned. Dark, glowing skin. Gold eyes. Stunning. "Yeah. Why?"

"Great. So who likes to bake?"

With a shy smile, Brooke was the first to raise her hand. Grinning even more broadly, Caitlin followed, then Micaela. The other two looked intrigued but skeptical.

"Dunno, I've never done it—"

"Me, either. Since Mom never lets me near *her* kitchen."

"Then, why don't we use the one here, bake some real cookies?"

"Or brownies?" Brooke said, and Caitlin high-fived her.

"Whatever you want. I'll buy the ingredients, we can have ourselves a baking party. Some for here, some to take home to your families. Because these things—" she waved the dirt cookie still in her hand "—need to die. Now."

That got an actual giggle from Miss Thirteen-Going-On-Twenty-Six. "Um…they're about to close…"

"Monday, then?"

After another shared glance, the girls muttered a chorus of "Sure, whatevers."

"Okay. Why don't you all find a recipe you'd like to make? You can use cookbooks or find something on the internet. Something not too complicated—"

"But if we've never baked before, how're we supposed to know if it's complicated or not?"

"Good point. So take out your phones." Four blinged-out phones duly appeared, and she gave them her number. "If you're not sure about the recipe, call or text me."

Jessica's green eyes zinged to Sabrina's. "You sure?"

"Absolutely."

"How's about we go to the store with you?" Micaela

said, her face practically glowing. "So we could get our own ingredients?"

"Actually, that's a great idea. Let's meet here at one on Monday. How's that?" When they all nodded, she said, "But give my number to your parents, have someone call me to make sure it's okay." She looked at their feet. "And wear comfortable shoes, we're going to be standing a lot—"

"Okay," Matt called out, clapping his hands. "Six o'clock! Equipment goes into the storage closet, windows locked, stray clothes picked up—you know the drill!"

Sabrina watched in amused silence as the girls tidied up, showing Brooke where the plastic storage containers were underneath the folding table, then dumping the plates of cookies into them...which shed light on one reason why the things were so awful: God alone knew how old they were.

Their chore done, the girls all thanked Sabrina—a couple even hugged her—waving goodbye to Brooke before clomping across the wooden floor toward the exit. Two of them were joined by a couple of the boys, although whether they were the girls' brothers or...something else, Sabrina had no idea. And wasn't sure she wanted to know, frankly.

"So that worked out well, huh?" she said to Brooke as they walked back toward Cole, standing by the door as kids swarmed past him like a river, laughing and talking.

"Yeah. It did." The girl flashed her a quick smile. "I really like Caitlin. And Shandra."

"Me, too. They seem like good kids."

"So how'd it go?" Cole asked, his eyes briefly touching Sabrina's before focusing on his daughter.

Brooke beamed. "The girls are pretty cool. Well, a couple of them, anyway. And we're going to get together and made cookies. With Sabrina."

"Sounds like fun."

"Doesn't it? Hey, Wes," she said as her brother approached, tossing Sabrina a look only marginally less toxic than the one from Jessica or whoever she was. His mistrust stung, no doubt about it. But, really, what did it matter, since she wasn't going to be in Maple River very long, anyway? And who knew where Cole and the kids would end up?

As Brooke launched into a play-by-play of the last half hour, Matt came up, tugging Sabrina's ponytail like they were still kids. Honestly.

"Those two remind me of us at that age," she said to her brother.

"Except you were never that nice to me," Matt said, and she smacked his arm. "It's true. Man, you were a major pain in the butt." He looked at Cole. "How the hell did you put up with her?"

"I'm not sure," Cole said, his gaze touching hers. Touching. Hell, *fondling*. Eesh. "Because your brother's right—"

"And now that we've settled that I was the devil's spawn," Sabrina muttered, wondering why, as she dug her car keys out of her pocket, Cole's honesty stung so much, "I guess it's time to head out—"

"And I need to get home before Kelly gets that *Oh, thank God* look on her face," Matt said. "But what is this about a baking party with the girls on Monday?"

"That's the plan, yep."

"You might want to check out the kitchen first," he said, backing away. "It's been a while since anyone used it. I can't vouch for how clean it is."

"Got it," she said, watching her brother walk away before frowning toward the other end of the vast room. Brooke came up beside her; without thinking, Sabrina slung her arm around the girl's shoulders.

"What is it?" Brooke asked.

Sabrina's gaze traveled upwards, scanning the huge space, eerily silent now that everyone had left. "When I was little, maybe six or seven, my mother brought me here one evening for some reason or other, I forget now. She got to chatting with someone, and like a doofus I wandered off to explore." Brooke giggled. "Got totally lost, couldn't find my way back. Ever since then…" She shrugged.

"The place gives you the creeps," Cole said, right behind her.

There wasn't even a trace of don't-be-silly derision in his voice. Only understanding. That soul-deep kindness she'd taken for granted so long ago…that made him the kind of man any woman would kill to partner with. Any sane woman, at least.

"Only when it's empty. Quiet like this."

"Yeah," Brooke said, her own voice hushed. "Like you can hear your breathing echoing."

Sabrina chuckled, the sound pinging off the rafters. "Exactly."

"You scared now?" Cole said, still kindly, and her throat clogged. But she shook her head, smiling down at Brooke.

"With you guys?" Her gaze glanced off Cole's. "Not a bit."

Liar.

"So where's this kitchen?" he asked.

"Through that door over there… What are you doing?"

"Expecting everybody to follow me. Come on, Wes, get your nose out of your phone and let's go exploring," he called, his voice booming through the empty space and sending those old fears scampering for cover.

To make room for new ones, only too eager to take their place.

Chapter Eight

By the time they'd determined the church kitchen wasn't in egregious violation of any health department code, everyone was starving. But when Brooke pleaded with Sabrina to join them at the local burger joint where they used to hang out in high school—and which still made the best burgers in Jersey, far as Cole was concerned—she'd begged off, insisting she was so tired after the long day she wasn't even hungry.

A big fat lie if ever he'd heard one. But probably just as well, since between his girl-child's glomming on to the woman and his son's obvious distrust—not to mention Cole's own conflicted feelings—spending more time together probably wasn't in any of their best interests.

That look she'd given him, back at the church…

Yeah. Meaning he guessed he wasn't the only conflicted one. Also, that all that unresolved crap was apparently going to remain unresolved, because that was life. His, hers, everybody's.

Even so, he thought as he knocked on his old bedroom door, interrupting Wes's Xbox gaming spree, he couldn't deny how good it felt to see Brooke smiling, to hear her laugh. Even if the reason for those smiles, that laughter, was only a jump-start. Not a permanent solution.

Hence the rampant ambivalence.

"Yeah?" Wes said, not taking his eyes off the small TV screen, assorted comatose pugs sprawled around him.

"Your hour's up, kid. Time to wind down and get ready for bed, anyway."

"Dad. I'm not a little kid. And it's summer—"

"And I'm not raising a vampire. Eleven is plenty late for a thirteen-year-old."

Clearly disgusted, Wes stabbed at the controller's buttons to exit the game, then tossed it on the floor, jerking awake the nearest dog. "I don't get it," he said as the dog stiffly rose, came over for reassurance. "Nana said you used to play Mario Brothers all the time when you were my age—"

"Not all the time, but far more than was good for me. Because I had no clue how to interact with actual human beings. Meaning my real life sucked. Not letting that happen to you."

Brandishing his best grump face, the kid slouched down in Cole's old beanbag chair—because his mother threw out nothing—his arms clamped across his chest. Yawning, the dog lay down again, immediately passing out once more. "Sounds like it didn't suck *that* much."

"Because I basically had no supervision whatsoever?"

"Well…yeah. You could do whatever you wanted, right? And anyway, if you hadn't played games so much, you probably wouldn't have been able to make up your own."

And the problem with having smart kids was…

"Maybe. But if I'd known then what I do now, I would've said the trade-off wasn't worth it. It's about balance, you know? The all-or-nothing approach rarely works out well, in the end."

"So why'd they let you do it?"

Feeling both out of his depth and grateful for being forced to learn how to swim, Cole sat on the edge of his old bed—complete with the same navy blue comforter— leaning forward with his elbows on his knees. "I think because they were both raised with too *many* rules. Lots of don'ts. So they didn't want that for Diana and me. They meant well," he said quickly, "but this whole parenting thing…" He sighed. "It's hard. No matter how much we don't want to screw it up, I think the odds are at least fifty percent we're going to, anyway."

"So…" A devilish smile pushed at the kid's mouth, much like the one he used to give as a toddler, when he'd grab something he wasn't supposed to have and take off with it, belly-laughing the whole time. "If that's the case…"

"No, you cannot stay up all night. Or play video games until your eyeballs fall out."

The kid shrugged. "It was worth a shot. But I still can't believe you actually admit you're…" He frowned.

"Human?"

"Yeah. That's it," Wes said, and Cole laughed. Then he sobered.

"Diana and I…we never really knew what was going on in our parents' heads. Not that they were deliberately keeping things from us as much as they never saw a reason to share."

"That is definitely not you," Wes said with a snorted laugh.

"I hope not, anyway. And I don't expect us to share every little secret with each other. I'll always respect your privacy. But if you need to talk things out—anything at all—I'm here. And I won't judge."

Not that he'd planned it that way, but he'd just given the kid an opening to talk about Sabrina. If he wanted to, that was. Since even Cole knew that any attempt to push the subject would most likely backfire. And why take that risk, when in a few weeks it would all be moot, anyway?

Wesley stretched out in the chair, his hands behind his head, his brow furrowed. "Did we just have one of those creepy parent-to-kid talks?"

"It would appear so," Cole said, getting to his feet, mildly disappointed that Wes hadn't taken the bait. "And, hey, nobody's head exploded."

"Not yet, anyway," his son said, and Cole smiled. Then Wes gave him a pointed look. "One question, though."

"Yeah?"

"If you played games so much you didn't know how to—what was it you said?—interact with other people? Then how'd you and Sabrina get to be such good friends?"

Cole's chest cramped. "Because she was pushy as hell," he said, thinking that would get a laugh from his son.

Instead, Wes's frown only deepened.

By the time Sabrina and the girls got to the church hall on Monday with their grocery-shopping loot for the Bake-a-Thon, she was both exhilarated and exhausted. And had sent up no less than a dozen prayers of gratitude to Jeanne Noble for her example in dealing with all those kids for so many years. But she was also grateful for the distraction after the way she and Cole had left things on Saturday. Honestly, her mumbled excuse for not going to dinner with him and the kids had probably sounded about as convincing as a D-list actor's performance in some SyFy Channel monster-meets-natural-disaster mash-up.

But what she'd heard in Cole's voice…speaking of mash-ups. Memories and longing and vulnerability, all smushed together in her brain. Loud and insistent, maybe, but far from real.

Or realistic.

The girls piled out of Pop's car, all talking at once. Even

Brooke, who she'd been grateful to see was getting on great with this mouthy, brassy, bodacious bunch. And yet, Sabrina heard—in their laughter and joking around, their unexpectedly respectful attitude toward her—old souls still harboring an innate innocence that no amount of makeup and borderline-trashy clothes and hard-assed attitudes could entirely quash.

A strength, whether the girls understood it or not, she could totally play to.

"Okay," she said when they reached the kitchen, which wasn't nearly as awful as her brother had led her to believe. The appliances, while not new, at least weren't decrepit; the counters were spacious, including a huge, stainless steel–topped island in the middle of the large room. And, hey, double ovens were double ovens, yo. As her chattering charges would say. "Everybody choose a counter space and set up all your ingredients. We won't be able to bake everything at once, but cookies don't take long, so those can go first."

"And then we can eat them while we're waiting for the other stuff to bake, right?"

This from Caitlin, natch. Who clearly wasn't going to keel over from starvation anytime soon.

"We can eat *some* of them," Sabrina said, setting the ovens to 350 degrees. "Because there is nothing better than cookies still hot and gooey from the oven." All the girls groaned. "But the whole point is sharing with the others, right?"

Brooke and one of the other girls had already started measuring out their ingredients into bowls Sabrina had lugged over from her father's house. Along with measuring utensils, wooden spoons, cookie sheets and assorted baking pans which she'd already decided to donate to the cause, since it wasn't as if her father was ever going to need this stuff. Or ever had. Baking was not part of his skill set.

She checked on each of the girls in turn, doling out only

that advice necessary to avert disaster. Or tears. Although Brooke had called to check if her macaroon recipe was too difficult—Sabrina had assured her it wasn't—Micaela had chosen to make some traditional Cuban sweet that involved a million ingredients and nearly as many steps. And while Sabrina admired the girl's ambition, she didn't hold out much hope for the recipe's ultimate success.

"Just remember," she said to the room at large after the first batches of cookies went in, "this is a learning process. If we mess up, we can try again. It took me I don't know how many tries to get my brownies right. Either they came out like cement, or so soft you needed to eat them with a spoon."

Brooke giggled. "So who taught you to cook?"

She smiled. "Jeanne Noble. The same woman who taught your dad. And my brothers—"

"Yo!" Shandra shrieked. "Get out of here!"

Sabrina spun around to see a couple of the boys standing at the kitchen door, dressed in various stages of baggy and grinning like loons as the girls all sent up an alarm like they'd been caught naked in the locker room.

"Sorry," said a black-haired dude with an abashed expression, his ball cap clutched in his hands. "But it smells so good, we couldn't focus on our game. Seriously, Mickie," he said when she rolled her dark brown eyes. "You guys making cookies and sh—stuff?"

"Maybe," she said, tilting her chin and with one hand on her hip, as another boy, then another and another crowded the doorway, noses twitching like hounds on a scent. Sabrina pressed her lips together to keep from laughing, flashing back to how the scent of her mother's baking would lure every young male in a ten-mile radius.

"You think maybe we could have some?" another boy asked, a shaggy blond who looked like some underfed waif straight out of *Oliver Twist*. Of course, that impression might have been due to his shirt being four sizes too large and his jeans crumpling around his ankles like a Shar-Pei's skin folds. His homies murmured their agreement, each one's eyes more pleading than the next. A smaller, dark-skinned boy dug into his equally baggy jeans pocket and pulled out a wad of very beat-up one dollar bills.

"We'll even pay," he said, and Sabrina's heart crumpled as badly as those pants.

"Don't be ridiculous," she said, "there's plenty. And we can always make more. So put your money back. In fact… you guys want to help?" Her eyes cut to the shocked/pissed/dumbfounded looks on the girls' faces, daring them to object, before swinging back to the boys. "I think we've got enough ingredients to make at least another couple batches of chocolate chip cookies."

"But we don't know how to do that."

"That's okay. We'll show you. Won't we, girls?"

Another laugh threatened to escape as her charges exchanged wide-eyed looks. Clearly, if any of this group had hooking up on the brain, showing a bunch of boys how to bake was not part of their plan.

And overseeing—she counted—eight boys in addition to the girls was definitely not part of hers.

As the boys ambled into the kitchen, Brooke came up beside her and whispered, "There's only one bag of chocolate chips left. And the flour and butter are almost gone, too."

"So, not enough stuff for eight additional people is what you're saying."

"Nope."

Crud. And she couldn't exactly leave them all unsupervised while she made a run to the store—

"You want me to call Dad?"

Oh, hell, no.

"Sure, sweetie. That would be great."

By the time Cole got to the church after stopping at the store, the whole block smelled like a cookie factory. Beeping his car locked, he headed inside the hall, the sounds of laughter and bickering and a throbbing salsa beat drawing him across the room to the kitchen. He had been busy, actually, debugging some codes for the new game he was developing. But he wasn't about to turn down a chance to get on Sabrina's good side.

Or her nerves. He wasn't picky.

Not that it would take much to accomplish that second thing, he thought when he first caught sight of her, her hair sloppily clipped on top of her head, trying to instruct three boys at once as they dumped what he assumed were chocolate chips into their bowls. What they weren't shoving in their mouths, that is.

Grinning, Cole came up behind her to whisper, "Cavalry's here. Also—" he unloaded two bags of flour, chips, butter and eggs on the table beside her "—supplies."

She twisted around to look up at him, gratitude beaming in her eyes. "Where's Wes?"

He wasn't about to tell her his son's reaction to the suggestion he tag along. "At home. Being thirteen."

Bree seemed to accept that. "Chocolate chip," she said, pointing to a couple of empty bowls—heavy, ceramic, one yellow, one green, both bearing the scars of his and Bree's youth. "You know what to do."

And indeed he did, having helped Bree and Kelly make God-knew-how-many batches of the things for every school, church or Scout fund-raiser Jeanne Noble got wind of. Even if it had been a while. It all came flooding back, though, the minute he picked up a bag of chips to read the recipe.

All of it, he thought with a glance at the woman whom he was guessing was currently straddling that very fine line between *having fun* and *frazzled*. Including—he looked away to find a pair of young men frowning up at him, their tough expressions and street-cred duds at such odds with their baby faces—tattered memories of kids who looked very much like this, whose mission in life had been to make his as miserable as possible. A life that would have been far more miserable if it hadn't been for Bree's presence in it.

That Cole should be in a position now to save her—not from bullying, no, but from the kids' almost suffocating enthusiasm…well. Guess irony had its humorous side, after all.

He told the boys to wash out the bowls, then bring them back over. Like males everywhere, they couldn't perform the simple task without annoying the hell out of each other, splashing and getting in each other's way, trading barbs at the speed of light.

As Cole watched, shaking his head, his gaze wandered to his daughter, smiling and laughing with the one with the massive hair, and his heart twisted.

Then he caught Bree watching him watching them, saw her smile in a way he hadn't for probably twenty years. A ghost, he thought, of that I-know-what-you're-thinking smile that'd signified a bond between them that had been real, and true, and, for a long time, indissoluble.

Except ghosts were nothing more than illusions, right? A trick of the light, perhaps. Of the imagination—

"Yo, Mr. Cole—we cleaned the bowls. So now what?"

"So now we make cookies. Only ours will be better than anybody else's."

"How come?"

He bent closer. "Extra chocolate chips," he whispered, which got a pair of grins. And high fives all around.

"Dude. Righteous," Marco, the shorter of the two, said, as Bree called out from the other side of the room, "What's going on over there?"

"Nothing," Cole shot back, and the boys chuckled, totally all about the subterfuge. And Cole laughed as well, totally in the moment.

Even if that's all it was—

He looked at Bree, radiating suspicion from across the room.

Or ever could be.

* * *

An hour later, Sabrina decided that, while in theory making a dozen kids clean had been the right thing to do, reality was something else again. Hence she and Cole were still washing up bowls and spoons and cookie sheets well after the last kid had trudged off—Brooke with Caitlin, to spend the afternoon—each with a container of goodies to share with his or her family. At one point, Father Bill had stuck his head in to see what was going on, surprise quickly giving way to delight. Especially when several of the kids insisted he sample the fruits—or baked goods—of their very loud labors. He may have even lifted his eyes to heaven. Not that Sabrina would have blamed him, having done a fair amount of sampling herself, blowing her carb allowance to hell and back in the process and not feeling the least bit guilty about it.

"Cookies," Cole said, snapping the top on to the last of the containers and tucking it into a locking cupboard. "Who knew?"

"I know, right?" She took a paper towel to a cookie sheet as Cole wiped down the stove, muscles shifting and bunching underneath a Henley shirt that could have been a size smaller, actually. "So much for makeovers and computer skills." Cole softly laughed, and she smiled, even though she still couldn't decide if she was glad he was here, or if she wished he would take his sexy, kind, funny, smart self away and leave her confused, frustrated, lonely self in peace.

"Thanks again for coming to the rescue. You were terrific with those boys. Showing them that real men bake cookies."

He shrugged. "Only being me."

"Which would be my point." More tired than she'd realized, Sabrina propped her elbows on the island, her hands folded in front of her. Easier on her back and a much better view. Might as well enjoy it, right? "The kids are damned lucky to have you as their dad," she said softly, and he whirled around. She expected him to argue. Instead, he smiled.

"Thank you. That means a lot, coming from you."

She blushed. And changed the subject.

"Did you have fun?"

"I did." He tossed her a smile. "And yourself?"

"Same here."

"So I take it you got over your anxiety?"

"More like they knocked it out of me."

"Truth," he said, waving the sponge at her before crossing to the sink to rinse it out. Setting the wrung sponge by the faucet, he turned around, swiping his damp hands down the back of his jeans. Which did fit. And quite nicely, too. "Which is why I'm guessing you agreed to a repeat performance next week?"

"It was like being set upon by a bunch of puppies. How could I not?"

His eyes crinkled when he grinned. "What I'm still a little vague on is how making more cookies turned into serving an entire meal."

"Father Bill gave me the idea, actually. When he said maybe they could sell the cookies to help with the roofing fund, it occurred to me—why *not* a dinner? For their parents? The congregation? Heck, the whole neighborhood? Admittance by donation, for really good spaghetti and garlic bread, salad, dessert. I'm sure enough people would pitch in to buy the food—Pop, for one. And I bet Kelly would help, too. Great way to get the kids involved, give them an opportunity to give instead of only receive all the time. A fund's all well and good, but it's so…impersonal. Something like this would bring everyone together, get them rallying around the cause—"

"It's a terrific idea, Bree," Cole said, in a way that warmed her all the way to her tootsies. "So the makeover idea…I take it that's been put to rest?"

"At least for now." Straightening, she walked around the island to hoist herself on to it, letting her legs swing. "Granted, a couple of them are over the top—or out of their tops—and I'm more than willing to take them shopping if their parents are on board. But, really, does it matter how they dress? They're just being themselves, you know?"

At his flummoxed expression, she smiled. "Thirteen's a rough age. As I'm sure you'll agree. But it's worse for girls, I think. You have no idea who you are, who you're *supposed* to be, how you're expected to act… I remember it well. And the fact that they're all wearing pretty much the same stuff tells me it's only a thing. A thing that'll pass. Like it always does."

"It doesn't bother you, the message they're sending?"

Only because she knew Cole so well—the old Cole, anyway—did she know he meant no offense. The dude didn't have a misogynistic atom in his body. If anything, he sounded genuinely concerned. But…

"I know what Matt said," she said quietly. "What he sees. What you obviously see, as well. But that combination of innocence and energy and street smarts…it touched something deep inside me. God knows they're not gonna take bubkes from nobody, but at heart they're all good girls. Pussycats, if you want to know the truth. Despite their tough-girl acts. At heart, no different than Brooke. Are some of them craving attention? Probably. Like I said, it's a rough time. But who am I to judge them by what they're wearing?"

Her face warmed. *Like I used to do to other kids when I was their age.* Shaking off the memory, she smiled. "And you know what else? Despite being outnumbered two to one by the dudes—some of whom were definitely making eyes at them—I didn't sense any of the girls were even remotely interested in returning the interest. Smart cookies, those gals."

Cole smiled. "At least smart enough to not go there with two adults in the room, maybe."

There was something about that smile, the barely banked laughter in his eyes, that sent a shudder through her entire midsection. And lower. Dammit. He'd always been intense, for sure. But adulthood had clearly focused that intensity with laser-like precision, and the result was...

Scary? Thrilling? Potentially devastating?

"Oh, trust me," she said, "if a girl wants to go down that road, there are ways without the grown-ups having a clue."

He paused, then said, "Speaking from experience?"

"Sadly, yes," she said on a sigh. With her hands braced on either side of her hips, she flexed her feet, stretching out her weary leg muscles. "Not saying I might not try to steer the girls toward clothes that are less...obvious, but I wouldn't dream of forcing the issue—"

One of her shoes clattered on to the linoleum floor, the noise like a gunshot. Sighing, she pushed herself off the table, losing her balance when she tried to wriggle her foot back into the shoe.

God, she really was tired, she thought, grabbing the edge of the island before she toppled over. Not too tired, however, to dodge Cole when he reached for her.

"No, I'm fine. Really," she said when his forehead crunched. Whether she was or not—at the moment, anyway—was beside the point. As was how attracted she was to him.

However.

It was well past time she stopped looking to other people—okay, men—to make her feel...whole. Because, one, hello? Illusion, much? And two, as long as she kept searching for something outside of herself to complete her, how the hell was she ever going to discover who she was? Yeah, it'd taken thirty-five years to figure this out, but figure it out, she had. Go, her—

"You really get off on kids, don't you?" Cole quietly asked, and she smiled.

"Yeah. I always have—"

His phone dinged. He tugged it out of his shirt pocket, tapped a brief reply, then replaced it. "Wes. Wondering where I am."

"Oh, crap, he probably is." *And God knows he doesn't need more reason to hate me.* "Please, go, I'll finish up, no problem—"

"Did I ever thank you? I mean, actually say the words, *Thank you*?"

Sabrina frowned. "For what?"

"Whatever else went down between us," he said quietly, capturing her gaze in his, "I will never, ever forget how you were a friend to me—a *real* friend—when nobody else gave a damn, whether intentionally or not. Even more than that…you *got* me. Like you get my daughter. Those girls. The way you…I don't know. Gain their trust. Same way you gained mine, a million years ago. That puts everything else into perspective. Because that soft heart inside a tough exterior thing? That's you to a tee."

"Soft? Cheah, right."

In no great hurry, Cole closed the distance between them, his *You will look at me* eyes making her breath hitch.

"W-why are you staring at me like that?"

Then, slowly, he smiled…and tapped her nose.

"Pussycat," he whispered, and walked away.

Chapter Nine

Standing at the stove browning ground beef—his son's lone cooking skill—Wes shot Cole what was probably supposed to be a withering look.

"What took you so long?"

Dogs smothered his calves, trying to glean the answer to that question through their noses. "There was a lot to clean up. And I couldn't leave Bree to do it all by herself. Whatcha making?"

"Tacos. Where's Brooke?"

"She went off with Caitlin."

"The one with the crazy hair?"

"Yep." Cole walked over and inhaled deeply, then pulled open a drawer for the ancient, but still serviceable, taco holders. "That smells great. I'm starved—"

"Mom called me."

He turned. "What? When?"

"While you were gone. Obviously." The kid stirred the meat one last time, then killed the flame under the burner. "She wants to get together. On Saturday."

"Here? Or Philly?"

"There. She said we could take the train, she'll meet us at the station."

"And that is not happening. I'll drive you." Wes glowered. "So sue me, I'm not letting you guys ride the train alone—"

"No, it's not that."

Cole frowned. "Don't you want to go?"

"Does it matter?"

"Of course it *matters*, Wes. If she wants to see you—"

"What she wants is to not feel guilty."

"You don't know that—"

"Considering she said how bad she feels, like, fifty times? Yeah. I do. So I'm guessing this isn't about wanting to see her own kids as much as it is making herself feel better about what she did."

"And again, you're not inside her head."

Tears flooded the boy's eyes, ripping Cole to pieces. Especially since he couldn't remember Wes crying since he was a toddler. "We don't even get to be alone with her, Dad," he said, his trying-to-change voice cracking. "She said we'll probably go to the zoo—like we're little kids, jeez—but that since her new boyfriend's never been, he's going with us."

Irritation spiked. "Oh?"

"Yeah. God, Dad, we haven't even seen her in two weeks, so you'd think…" His lower lip quivering, Wes turned back to the stove. "But just like always, we're not enough."

Cole wished like hell he could refute the kid's statement, but considering why they were living with him to begin with, how could he? He thought about Bree, how everything about her softened when she'd talked about "her" girls…kids she barely knew, for heaven's sake. He could only imagine what she'd be like with her own—

He took a deep breath. "She say what this guy's name was?"

"I think, yeah, but…sorry, I don't remember. I wasn't really hearing too clearly by that point."

No, Cole didn't imagine so. He did, however, foresee a chat with his ex in the near future. Was the woman really that selfish? Or simply clueless as crap? And what did it say about him, that after nearly fifteen years, two kids and a divorce, he didn't know the answer to that?

He walked over to his son to clamp a hand around the back of the kid's slightly sweaty neck and tug him close, his heart melting all over again when, instead of pulling away—which Cole would've expected—Wes hugged him back.

"I'll talk to your mom," he said quietly, and Wes nodded against his chest, then sucked in a shaky breath that sliced straight through Cole. Releasing a none-too-steady breath of his own, he backed up enough to look into his son's eyes.

"But I want you to know…you guys are definitely enough for me. In fact, you're everything." Which he'd best remember for the foreseeable future. "You got that?"

After a moment, Wes nodded again, then pulled away to shred the block of cheese sitting on the counter, swiping his forearm across his nose. Sighing, Cole yanked off a paper towel, handed it to him.

"Thanks," the kid muttered, blowing.

"Sure."

"Um…I made iced coffee?"

"A man after my own heart," Cole said, and his son's grin turned him inside out.

Fortunately, this thing called life kept Sabrina from having to interact with Cole or his kids over the next little while—overseeing the rest of the staging for her father's house, schlepping into the city a couple of times for appointments, babysitting her nieces and nephew so Kelly and

Matt could have date night. Didn't keep her from thinking about them, however.

All of them, she thought, as she and her part-time assistant lugged bulging dress bags through the lobby of a swanky East Side apartment building.

She thought about Brooke's smiles as she bonded with the other girls. Her hugs, wrapping around Bree's heart as well as her waist. Wes's glares that first day at the center. His rampant distrust. Cole's coming to her rescue with the cookie baking... The way his pupils dilated when he approached her, there at the end. That tap on her nose. Especially that tap on the nose. Which, really, wasn't even in the least bit erotic.

Really.

However, it didn't matter how sweetly that laugh or those eyes or the smell of him sang to her libido, her tatteredbatteredsplattered ego. The issues with Wes aside, she was in major rebound mode. Signs of which she knew all too well. Only this time she was determined to actually *pay attention to them.* Instead of dragging some poor dude—and his kids—into the abyss with her.

"Hey. Sabrina." Smushed into the elevator with the bags, she looked at her assistant, Frankie, an aspiring actress who was only too happy to pick up a few extra bucks by playing pack mule now and again. "You've said like two words to me since we left Bloomie's. What gives?"

"Sorry, sweetie. Lots on my mind, that's all. It's not you."

"Yeah? Oh." The girl made a face. And she didn't even know the half of it. "Right."

The apartment was on the twenty-third floor. Great view. Long-ass ride to get there. Shifting the heavy bag in her arms, Sabrina rested her head against the burled-maple paneling, shifting a little to smile for the shaggy-haired blonde. Bright purple leotard, denim vest, yellow leggings, short checked skirt, vintage Jimmy Choo pumps.

In silver. More holes in her body than a sieve. *This could be Brooke in a few years,* came the unbidden thought, and she shuddered.

Not that she'd ever know.

"Actually, I'm okay," Sabrina said as the elevator gently bumped to a stop on their floor and they shuffled across black-and-white-checkered marble to the double-paneled doors leading to the sole apartment on the floor. "It's been good, being back in New York." The lights and noise, the perpetually comforting thrum of energy, embracing her like that in-your-face but much-beloved friend each time she returned. "Can't wait until I can ditch the commute, though."

"And I told you," Frankie said, "you're welcome to crash with me—"

"That's very sweet, really. But I think my roomie days are behind me."

"But the deposit and everything on a place of your own…?"

"Getting there." Even if not as fast as she might've hoped.

"Whatever. If Jersey begins to drive you crazy, the offer stands."

Begins? Another conversation like that with Cole, and she'd be certifiable—

A smiling, Chanel-perfumed Gilda Rabinowitz opened the door, ushering them inside as though they were visiting royalty. Clasping her hands in front of her flat chest, Gilda sucked in a breath at the sight of the bags.

"Ooooh…those look promising…"

Two upcoming weddings, three charity functions, and a few pieces to "freshen" up a wardrobe enjoying the high life in a cedar-lined walk-in closet larger than Sabrina's first apartment. Insane. But, hey, if it paid the bills…

Or, in this case, enabled her to get away from a pair of sexy silver eyes…not to mention a pair of kids who needed more than a mother-of-convenience…

Her phone signaled an incoming text. As Frankie hung the clothes on a portable garment rack, Sabrina dug the phone out of her purse, her breath catching in her throat when she read it.

"What?" her assistant whispered. Sabrina turned the display toward her. Heavy brows shot up.

"Dude," she whispered. "You gonna do it?"

"Why not?" she said brightly, leaving Frankie to shake her head as Sabrina quickly texted back, Sure thing, see you then, to the woman who'd come within a hairbreadth of becoming her mother-in-law.

"Can't quite believe it myself," the Colonel said, flipping first one, then the other steak on the old charcoal grill. "But the first open house is on Sunday. Not expecting anything right away, of course. This isn't some TV show, after all. And the market being what it is…"

The sentence left dangling, the older man picked up his can of soda from the attached tray on the grill and joined Cole, lowering himself into the newly cushioned iron chair across from his. Out in the neatly trimmed yard, where Jeanne Noble's roses reveled in the mid-July humidity, the pugs romped and yipped, all grinning their little puggy grins. The invitation had been a surprise. But the older man said he wanted to give the old grill one last whirl before the for-sale sign went back up. And everybody else had plans.

"Or, as they call them, lives," he'd said with a grunt, and again Cole found himself hard-pressed to refuse the invitation.

"So. Anyway," Sabrina's father said. "Glad you came. Sorry the kids aren't here, though."

"Me, too."

Preston frowned. "You worried about them going with their mother?"

"Now that we've ironed out the details?" Cole said with a tight grin. "No." He'd given Preston a recap, including how he'd basically shamed his ex into seeing her kids without a tagalong boyfriend who probably wouldn't last the month. His finest moment, no. But a father does what he's gotta do. And right now—okay, forever—it was all about the kids. What was best for them, not what was convenient for the grown-ups.

The upshot was, Erin had driven to Maple River—alone—to pick them up for the whole weekend, promising it would only be the three of them the entire time. Brooke, bless her heart, was thrilled. Wes, however, was skeptical. Understandably enough.

"I do miss the little stinkers, though," he now said with a half smile. "Funny, how used you get to having them around."

"Yeah," Preston said on a pushed breath, and Cole saw the loneliness in the older man's eyes. That unsettled feeling of not being sure what came next. A feeling Cole knew all too well.

"Wasn't Bree supposed to return tonight?"

The Colonel pushed himself to his feet to poke at the steaks, sending their mouthwatering smoke across the yard and to the dogs over at the patio, tongues lolling.

"She was. But she got an unexpected appointment for tonight."

Cole somehow doubted Bree had thought of Maple River as home for years. He, however, had no problem acknowledging that he was not a city person. Not even after living in Philly. Or maybe because of it. The thought of making his home in crowded, smelly, noisy New York made his skin crawl—

"What?" he said, suddenly catching a word or two of what the Colonel was saying.

"The client. It's Chad's mother. Kathryn. Who introduced them, actually. Did you know that?"

Cole shook his head. After their initial, not-exactly-detailed conversation about what had brought her back to

Maple River, the subject hadn't come up again. Not that he'd expected it to.

"Nice enough gal, I suppose, although we've only met once. The engagement party, at the Davies's place out on the Island. Anyway…" The Colonel moved the steaks to a serving platter, shut the lid on the grill. "So she called. I could tell, Sabrina was surprised. You know, given the situation and all. But that's where she is tonight. Out on the Island."

"With her ex's mother?"

"Yep. Um…I bought some rolls and potato salad from the supermarket, some bagged salad. That good enough for you?"

"Of course, it's fine." Cole rose from his chair, the older man's words roiling in his brain. "It's certainly better than whatever I would have scrounged up."

"Everything's in the fridge. Why don't you go grab them? And some plates and utensils, too, while you're at it."

Once inside, Cole yanked open the fridge, staring blankly inside. Then he shut it. Opened it again, grabbed the bagged greens, the tub of potato salad.

Then he dug his phone from his pocket.

Texted Bree.

Having dinner with ur dad. He told me where u were. U OK?

He'd just dumped the greens into a bowl when his phone dinged.

1—Write in real English. And 2—Why wouldn't I be?

He smiled. And texted back:

Because it can't be easy.

A search for salad dressing turned up a single, nearly empty bottle of old-school French. Shaking his head, he loaded everything on a tray—

It's not.

Then why r

He backspaced.

Then why are you doing it?

Because the breakup had nothing to do with her.

A second passed.

Also, she pays well.

Like, VERY well.

"Cole? What's the holdup, son?"
"Be right there!"

So this is only about money?

He stared at the screen, waiting.

It's my job, Cole. And some of us can't afford to be choosy. Gotta go, the Davies are taking me out to dinner. TTYL.

He hauled everything outside, and they tucked in, Cole's attention wandering as they worked their way through steaks a little underdone for his taste. Suddenly he realized Preston had stopped talking, instead watching him intently as he chewed.

"Sorry," Cole muttered, with what he hoped was an apologetic smile. "Lot on my mind."

"About the kids?"

"Among other things, yeah."

"Like my daughter?"

And how the hell was he supposed to answer that?

"I—"

But Preston held up a hand, then said softly, "You probably have no idea, the look on your face when I bring up her name. Which pretty much matches the look on hers when I talk about you." Then he sighed. "Would somebody please tell me why you young people make everything so damned complicated?"

Because it was. That's why.

For a moment, Sabrina thought her eyes were tricking her when the train pulled into the station, and she saw, through the grimy window, Cole standing on the platform, all hunky and such in khaki shorts and a knit shirt that actually fit. And dammit, her empty stomach went kaflooey. Especially since, after the excruciatingly boring, nearly two-hour trek that always left her ready to chew her arm off, anyway, this was the last thing she needed.

"Hey," he said softly when they met, and *No!* and *Oh, yeah* clashed inside her head like a pair of cymbals. "Glad to be back?"

Looking at him as if he was speaking Sanskrit, Sabrina hiked her supersize tote bag up on to her shoulder. "Since every time I do, I feel as though I've left part of myself in New York, I'm gonna say no to that."

Never mind that the whole time she'd been in the city, she'd also felt as though she'd left part of herself in Jersey. So sad.

"So, what are you doing here?" She looked behind him. "Alone?"

Cole reached for her bag, then started toward the stairs

leading down to the parking lot. "The kids are with their mother. And your dad asked me to pick you up."

Speaking of thoughts colliding in her head.

"What?" she said, following him. Trying not to gawk at his calves.

"Apparently Erin remembered she had kids. And your dad got sucked into emergency babysitting—"

"Ohmygod! Is everything okay?"

"Kelly's son broke his wrist or something? And Matt's at work. But, yes, to answer your question." They reached his car; he opened the door for her, giving off a whiff of yummy man-scent that sent her hormones into a feeding frenzy. "So how'd it go?"

At least by the time they'd both gotten into the front seat she'd recovered enough to say, "By 'it' I assume you mean the Long Island side trip?"

"Uh-huh."

"It was fine. No, really. I like Kathryn. Tom, too. He's totally down-to-earth and she's a great client, doesn't treat me like the hired help—hell, she doesn't treat the hired help like the hired help—and nobody mentioned the elephant in the room. We were all on our best behavior, you would have been proud."

Cole regarded her a second or so too long before putting the car in gear and pulling out of the station's parking lot. "That the truth?"

"Okay, so things were a little dicey. Because I could tell how disappointed they were. Are. That things didn't pan out between me and their son. But whatcha gonna do? So. How was dinner with Pop? Or should I say, *why* was dinner with Pop?"

He pulled on to the main highway that would take them back to Maple River. "Working backward, because he asked. And, to use your own word, fine." He paused. "This transition…I don't think it's easy for him. Which is probably why I think he has matchmaking on the brain."

"Oh, yeah? And who's the lucky couple?"

Cole tossed her an amused glance before refocusing on the road. "Us, goofball." At her silence—because her brain refused to cough up a coherent thought, let alone verbalize it—he said, "I thought you should know. Forewarned and all that."

"Um, thanks? But…" She frowned. "Why?"

"I'm guessing he wants you to stick around. So…" He shrugged.

"Except you don't even know if you are. Right? So it doesn't even make sense."

"This isn't about logic, Bree. It's about…" One hand on the steering wheel, he pressed the other to his chest. And her own cramped.

Sabrina sighed. "Everybody else is right here, for heaven's sake. Why does he think he needs me, too?"

"Because you're not everybody else," Cole said quietly.

And then let that sit there.

So, before her brain exploded into a million gooey bits, she said, "Well, here's hoping once he gets settled in at Sunridge, things will be better." Then she grinned. "Maybe we should try to fix *him* up. It'd serve him right. All those widow ladies over there…" She snapped her fingers. "Hey—how about your aunt?"

"Lizzie?" Cole chuckled. "Other than the fact that she's old enough to be his mother? She'd eat him alive."

"You don't think Pop could handle her?"

"I don't think Godzilla could handle her," he said, and she laughed. And God, it felt so good to laugh. To be with someone she could simply be herself around—

"That necklace…wow. Is it new?"

"What? Oh." She fingered the turquoise and coral bib necklace lying heavily against her breastbone. "I picked it out for Kathryn a couple of years ago, but she says it's too much of a statement piece to wear anymore. So she asked me if I wanted it."

"I'm guessing that's not from Target."

"Good call. But they've got money to burn, and as long as she keeps spending it, she helps keep the economy going. And, yes, it occurred to me that there might've been a wee bit of guilt coloring the offer. At least I got a kick-ass necklace out of the deal, right?"

Cole shot her an unreadable look, then said, "So I take it you knew Chad came from money when you started going with him?"

Sabrina hadn't expected the question to hit as hard as it did. Or for as many reasons. "Since his mother introduced us, yeah. Obviously. Why?"

"Just wondering."

A beat or two passed before the light dawned. "And I cannot believe you'd even suggest that I'd marry someone for his money—"

"I wasn't—"

"Although I can certainly see where you might worry about people cozying up to you more because of what you had than who you were. That it might even make someone not want to tell their oldest friend about, say, a game they'd developed that had made them a small fortune? Or maybe not so small, I don't know."

Cole gripped the wheel, then released a breath. "Diana, right?"

"Yep. And I can't tell you how proud I am of you. But there was a moment when I wanted to clobber you, too, that you didn't feel you could trust me—"

"I don't tell anyone about my money, Bree. Not so much because it's none of anyone's business—although it isn't—but because it simply doesn't occur to me. Since having it doesn't change who I am. I'm still the same dweeb I was before, so it all feels…irrelevant, I suppose. I wasn't afraid to tell you. And of *course* I trust you, so you can put that thought right out of your head." His gaze glanced off hers. "I simply didn't think it would matter. Not between us."

Sabrina looked out the windshield again, her eyes stinging for reasons that, really, had nothing to do with them. Even so...

"So why'd you bring up the subject?"

A second or two passed before Cole said, "Because too many people confuse money with happiness. Or the stuff it can buy with being there for the people they supposedly love."

"And I said—"

"For cripes sake, Bree—I'm not talking about you! So would you get off your high horse, already? What I meant was..." He sighed. "Look, I don't know this dude from Adam. Or what his motive was in wanting to marry you. But a lot of these guys, they see women as, well, prizes. No, wait, let me finish—you said things hadn't felt right between you for a long time. And, yes, I know what you said, about his kid. But maybe there was more to it than that. Maybe...okay, here's my theory. Maybe this Chad person eventually realized you didn't fit into his plan. Because you're far too much your own person to ever be bought. So the money issues...they were on his side. Not yours."

Now her eyes burned for an entirely different reason. One that had everything to do with them. "You've obviously been giving this a lot of thought."

"You might say."

Sabrina knuckled away a tear poised to escape, then cleared her throat. "It wasn't like that," she said carefully, still not entirely trusting her voice. "I swear. But..." Blinking, she glanced out her window, then back at him. "Nobody's ever said anything like that to me before. No guy, anyway."

After the mother of all pregnant pauses, his eyes touched hers. "So we're good?"

"Sure. Although if we ever go out to eat? No way in hell am I suggesting we go Dutch."

Chuckling, he reached over and squeezed her forearm,

his touch warm and firm and lovely, and her dozing hormones jerked awake like a dog hearing the fridge open. "You got it." Then he grinned. "So…what was that you were saying about being proud of me…?"

God, he was so cute it hurt. "You have no idea, whenever I see somebody playing the game, the restraint it takes to not get up in their grill and say, 'My friend did that!' But that would be tacky." Her gaze slid to his. "It would, right?"

"Absolutely," he said. But with that look people got when you've said exactly the right thing.

"And you know something else?" she said before her heart oozed right out of her chest, "I'd give my right arm to see the faces of all those jerkwads in school who gave you a hard time." She snorted. "Who are the losers now, huh?"

A long moment passed before he said, very quietly, "Thanks."

"De nada."

And that should have been the signal to the universe, as they zipped past a conglomeration of big-box stores and chain restaurants, to let them settle into a silence far more comfortable than it was. Instead, whatever this was shimmering between them reminded her of a time that had practically burgeoned with unanswered questions and thwarted desires. Almost as if the more they got out in the open, the more there was underneath. An emotional Pandora's box.

Hoping to slam the lid on that sucker, Sabrina asked, "So you said the kids are with their mom?"

"Yeah," Cole sighed out.

"This is a good thing, no?"

"Wish I knew. Brooke seemed happy enough to go with the flow, but her brother isn't as forgiving as she is. Or as trusting. Far as he's concerned, she screwed them over."

"He is only thirteen," Sabrina said softly, wondering why she'd thought this would be a *safer* topic.

"Yeah, well, I'm thirty-five, and I'm inclined to agree with him."

As she was saying. Thinking, anyway.

"You don't believe people deserve a second chance?"

No sooner were the words out of her mouth than Sabrina realized what she'd said. And who she'd said it to. As had Cole, apparently, judging from his very quiet "Of course" in response, and her face flamed. "I'd be a pretty big hypocrite if I didn't. But these are my kids we're talking about. And Erin hurt them pretty badly. If you'd heard Wes the other night, after she called…"

He shook his head, his jaw clenched. "Obviously I want them to have a relationship with their mother. But only if it's a healthy one. I know what they say about kids being resilient and all, but…"

"But this age is hard enough when everything's boringly stable," Sabrina said, looking at the cars in front of them. "I get it."

She felt his gaze on the side of her face. "Do you?"

Something told her there were more layers to that simple question—to this conversation—than her mother's homemade strudel. Shifting in her seat, she fingered the heavy necklace. But the weight crushing her chest had nothing to do with a bunch of metal and stones.

"After Abby was born, my folks didn't take on many fosters. But there were a couple, around that age, who'd been through the mill. Abused, abandoned, you name it. And I remember Mom and Pop doing everything they could to make them feel safe. To make their world stop spinning."

Now she faced his profile as he drove. "So, yeah. I get it. Especially that, for a child? There aren't degrees of suckage. Pain is pain. And as their dad, you'll do anything you can to make the pain stop."

He reached across the console again to squeeze her hand. And this time, her hormones stayed blessedly asleep.

Because she knew, now more than before, that the very thing that made him the best man she'd ever known—aside from her brothers and father—was also the very thing that would keep them from making even a more stupid mistake than they'd made the first time.

And eventually, she might even be grateful for that.

Chapter Ten

If he'd had his druthers, Cole would have avoided the big church fund-raising dinner the following Friday like the plague. Especially after that car ride with Sabrina. Frankly, he thought as he drove through the gates to his aunt's complex, he was surprised the irony hadn't killed him dead on the spot. Because over and over, all he could think about was her compassion and empathy and sense of justice, that soul-deep goodness that had only ripened along with the rest of her...

Her sense of humor, he thought, smiling.

Dammit, she couldn't be a more perfect mom for his kids.

Only, with everything they were going through with their mother—whose good intentions had apparently been short-lived, her inattention to the kids over the weekend leaving Brooke depressed and confused and Wes even angrier—the last thing they needed was someone new tossed into the mix. Even if that someone was Sabrina.

Especially if that someone was Sabrina, who'd been through enough crap of her own in the past little while.

Complex gaming codes, he could figure out, no problem. His life? Not so much.

The instant Cole's great-aunt opened her front door, her blue-lidded eyes scrunched up behind her glasses. "And don't you look like crap on a cracker."

"Hello to you, too, Lizzie," he said, leaning over to peck the old girl on her withered cheek as the breeze from the open patio door made her caftan ripple around her. "I was up all night trying to debug a new game." A lie, but whatever. "And thanks for doing this."

Not that his aunt had any intention of showing up to the dinner herself, but she was all for preserving such a lovely example of late nineteenth-century architecture. So she'd volunteered to contribute to the cause in the form of her killer spinach dip. Swatting at him, she stiffly stalked off to the tiny kitchenette wedged into one corner of the living room, awkwardly hauling a large crystal bowl out of her fridge. "You alone?"

Cole quickly relieved her of the heavy, deeply etched bowl. She seemed grateful. "Wes and Brooke are already at the church, with Kelly." Who'd been only too happy to supervise the meal, as well the dozen or so kids who'd eagerly volunteered to help. "And again, this is very generous of you."

"My pleasure. Just make sure the bowl gets back to me. Belonged to my mother. Only thing of hers I got left. Heavy, right? Would hurt like a sonofabitch if it should happen to come in contact with your head." He frowned at her as she handed him a box of Ritz crackers to go with. "Girl troubles is what I'm thinking. And let me take another swing at it—it's that Sabrina. The cutie you used to hang out with when you two were kids."

"I don't—"

"These new glasses, they're something else. I got like

X-ray vision now. Like I didn't see you looking at her at the wedding. And I think, huh. Because I remember that look from before." Her mouth turned down at the corners. "Then I think about you and Erin, about how badly that turned out. No, you never said anything about it, but your mother did. Your sister. And you can shut your mouth right now. They love you. They worry. Like family's supposed to."

She reached over, rested her delicate hand on his wrist. "You're a good boy, Cole. You deserve better. You deserve…" Her brow puckered. "You deserve whatever the hell you want. And so do those two great kids."

Lizzie had always had an uncanny ability to zero in on a person's thoughts, but this was surreal even for her. "Yeah, well…it's not that easy."

"So, what is? You want the good stuff in life, you gotta go after it. 'Cause sure as hell it ain't gonna come to you. So. Is this gal worth the trouble? You tell me."

Giving in—or up, hard to tell—Cole sat on the edge of Lizzie's gold brocade sofa, balancing the bowl on his lap. "Okay, for one thing? She's just come off a two-year relationship—"

"Better than still being in one." The loose garment billowed around her legs as she toppled into the upholstered chair across from him. "Go on."

"*Just* come off, Lizzie. As in, still hurting. And not looking." His aunt shrugged. *No big deal.* "But even more important…"

He explained about the kids and their mother. How emotionally tender they were, too.

"Uh-huh," Lizzie said, then squinted. "So why do you love this woman?"

"Didn't say—"

"Hey. Old, yes. Stupid, no."

"Not so sure about that, since you clearly didn't hear a thing I said."

Clearly unoffended, his aunt swatted at him. "I heard what I needed to, trust me. Well?"

He could lie, he supposed. To himself as well as the squinty-eyed woman in front of him. But what would be the point?

Other than self-preservation, that is.

"Because she's funny and tough and has, like, the biggest heart of anyone I've ever known. Because…the world's simply a better place when she's around. Still crazy, God knows. And not perfect. And it's making *me* crazy…" He pushed out a sigh. "That I can't see how to make this work."

"With the kids, you mean?"

"All of it. Her, the kids, the timing…logistics aren't exactly working in our favor, here."

Lizzie lowered her eyes to her veiny hands, tightly folded on top of her knees, before lifting them to Cole again.

"I never had kids—wanted them, but it never worked out—so I've got no business telling you what to do on that score. Although I'd like to slap that Erin into next week. *But* I do think you're not giving them—or yourself—enough credit, for being able to acclimate more than you think they can. Yeah, I get it, you want to protect them, give them time to adjust. You're a good father. A good *man*. But, honey, when you find someone who makes you feel like Sabrina obviously makes you feel…" Slowly, she shook her head. "You don't let go of that for anything. Because if you do, you'll regret it for the rest of your life."

Cole frowned. "You…?"

"A million years ago, yeah. In my case, it was the guy's sister. She had developmental issues, I think that's the right term these days. Greatest guy ever. In part because he *was* so devoted to his sister." Her eyes got watery. "But he couldn't see how it would work, either. Said it wouldn't be fair to me. And I was young enough—and dumb enough—to believe him. So we called it off. And it kills me to this day that I didn't fight for him. For us. For what we could've had."

Then Lizzie slapped her hands on her knees and stood, clearly meaning their little chat was over. As she walked him to the door, though, she laid her hand on his arm, making him look down into those frighteningly wise eyes.

"Being cautious is for wimps, Cole. And you're no wimp." She smiled. "You never have been, whether you believe that or not. Maybe what this Sabrina needs is somebody who *will* fight for her. Someone with the cojones not to let anything get in his way. Now get outta here, I got things to do…"

Cole heard his great-aunt's front door clunk shut as he climbed behind the wheel, carefully setting the bowl and crackers in the passenger side well before straightening.

Then he chuckled—maybe if the old gal had been more a part of his life all along, he would've been a little less boneheaded about a few things. But now her words rang loud and clear, giving him a much-needed and woefully well-deserved kick in the pants.

Because, as with a video game, so with real life: there was no getting to the next level without taking some risks. Overcoming obstacles. Which, in this case, were legion.

Then again, how much fun would the game be if it were easy?

Time to dust off those cojones, he thought, grinning, as he backed out of the parking space and headed for the church.

"Does this look clean enough?" Brooke asked after the church dinner, frowning at the kitchen's island.

Sabrina smiled. Pretty much everyone else had gone home, but Cole had insisted he and the kids stay and help clean up. Brooke had eagerly volunteered for kitchen duty while Wes and Cole were still in the main hall, putting away long-unused tables and chairs.

"Does to me," she said as she dried the industrial-sized pots and pans they'd used to make the spaghetti. "You ready to join the others?"

"In a sec. I need to use the bathroom first."

"Okay, I'll meet you by the stairs?"

"Deal."

Seconds later Sabrina sank onto the last riser, releasing a weary but satisfied sigh as she watched Cole and Wes on the other side of the hall load folding chairs onto a rolling cart. On so many fronts, the event had been a huge success, from how it had brought the community more together than it had been in years, to how much money it'd raised. More than anyone could have imagined, according to Father Bill. Including one large, anonymous donation… as if Sabrina couldn't figure out the donor's identity. Especially since a brand-new, state-of-the-art computer had also magically appeared in the church office, she thought on a smile when Cole laughed at something Wes said, his eyes so full of love for the kid it made Sabrina's heart hurt.

Hurt more, that is.

Because on a personal front, things were basically a mess. Bad enough that every time she saw Cole, she thought, *Yes, please.* Especially when she'd catch him looking at her and see the same thing in his eyes. Except she'd thought that before, hadn't she, with other men? Nice men, *good* men, men she'd seen a future with.

Yeah.

And that wasn't even taking into consideration Cole's children, who were ripping her apart inside. Brooke…oh, God—dear, sweet Brooke, making Sabrina fall in love with her even though she knew she shouldn't…and scowly, intense Wesley, every bit as sensitive as his father had been at that age, determined to guard his heart for the same reason his sister so eagerly gave hers.

And, boy, could Sabrina relate to both of them. Except in this case, it wasn't only about protecting herself, it was about protecting two kids who didn't need any more question marks in their lives. Or at least deserved a break from them.

She heard Brooke's footsteps behind her before the girl came around to join her on the stairs, plunking her skinny little butt on the step above Sabrina's.

"Sorry my brother's being such a pain," she said, and Sabrina was glad the girl couldn't see her face.

"If it's any consolation," she said, "so were my brothers at that age. Well, except for maybe Ethan. The oldest. But then, the rest of us often wondered if he was an alien. One trying way too hard to be the perfect human."

"Not something anybody can ever say about Wes, that's for sure." Then Brooke sighed. "Did Dad tell you about our weekend with Mom?"

"Only that you went. How was it?"

"It sucked. Like, seriously."

Feeling as though her chest would cave in, Sabrina reached back to wrap her hand around Brooke's. "I'm so sorry, sweetie."

"I don't get it. I mean, I know Wes and I were both—" she made air quotes "—'accidents,' but if Dad can deal with it, why can't she?"

"What makes you think…?"

"Mom doesn't exactly keep her voice down when she's on the phone."

Not my place to judge, not my place—

"Well," Sabrina said gently, "to be honest, a lot of kids aren't exactly planned." She chuckled. "My baby sister was a huge surprise—"

"Yeah, and some surprises are good, and some aren't," she said, and Sabrina thought, *Oh, dear God.* "And it's not like I don't think Mom loves us. In her own way, I guess. But for sure not like Dad does. The way he looks at us, talks to us…there's a difference, you know?" She huffed a sigh. "I can't explain it. But we can feel it. Does that make any sense?"

"It makes perfect sense. Because that's kind of the way it was with my parents. My birth parents, I mean. Matt and I always knew our mother loved us, but our father…" She shook her head. "Although that's not a fair comparison, really, because my father…he wasn't very nice."

The girl slid down to sit on the step beside Bree. "Like, he hurt you guys?"

"Not me. But my mother and Matt, yeah."

"Wow. You're right, Mom's not *that* bad. But still. I don't think we realized how different they were when we were little—probably because we were with Mom more. So I guess we thought that's just how things were. Only then we overheard that phone call."

"When was this?"

"Right before we asked to go live with Dad. It was like one of those games where you have to keep stacking blocks or whatever until it all falls down? Hearing Mom say that stuff…that was the last block. But…" The girl's gaze touched Sabrina's. "Don't get me wrong, the way Mom is, it hurts me, too. That she, like, abandoned us. But I think it hurts Wes more."

Dimly, Sabrina remembered conversations she and Cole had had at about that age, after they'd first met. How being around Sabrina and her close-knit family had made him realize how disconnected he'd felt from his parents. The kid was clearly her father's child. Which certainly didn't make Sabrina love her—and no doubt about it, she did love her—*less*.

"Have you said any of this to your dad?"

"Oh, yeah. Because he makes us talk about it." Her mouth pulled to one side. "Whether we want to or not."

"Still. It's good, having someone who wants to listen."

"I guess," Brooke said, but with a little grin.

"So we're all done here," Cole said, coming up to them.

Wes hung back slightly, his hands slugged into his shorts pockets, wearing the same mulish expression Sabrina had come to think of as normal. "Who's up for ice cream?"

Sabrina wasn't sure who was more surprised, she or Wes…whose face, when his gaze swung to his father, was so comical she nearly laughed out loud.

"At that place we passed after we parked?" Brooke said, popping to her feet.

"Why not?" Cole turned to Sabrina. "You in?"

"You mean…Antonio's?"

"Yep."

She hadn't even thought of the old diner in years, where she and Kelly and Cole used to hang out when they got tired of fighting the crowds at Murphy's. The burgers had been terrible, but the ice cream sundaes and milk shakes had been the stuff of dreams.

"Say yes," Brooke said, her eyes bright as she grabbed Sabrina's hand in both of hers. A little girl, still, inside what she'd come to realize was an old, wise soul. And Sabrina's own soul ached in response.

Especially when she caught Cole's gaze, brimming with memories. And more. Much, much more. The kind of more that might make some girls believe in fairy tales again—

Some girls. Not her.

Squelching a sigh, Sabrina dared a glance at Wes, whose gaze briefly touched hers before veering away. And it wasn't that she didn't understand his turmoil, probably more than he did. The confusion, the sense of betrayal… She got it. Even so, it was beginning to annoy the hell out of her, his refusal to believe she was no threat. He didn't have to like her—especially since she wasn't going to be a permanent part of their lives, a thought that pinched a lot more than she might have expected—but she did want him to feel he could trust her.

And that wasn't going to happen if she bolted every time the kid got ticked off.

"Ice cream sounds great," she said, and Brooke squealed out a "Yes!" as her brother sighed…

And Cole stood there grinning like a doofus.

A grin that made her melt faster than ice cream on a summer's night.

They let the kids go ahead, the two of them talking quietly between themselves as they meandered along the darkening, uneven sidewalk. Built on the farthest edge of their old stomping grounds, All Saints anchored an older, mainly blue-collar area once inhabited by factory workers, service-sector types, those intrepid souls with the chutzpah to start their own businesses—the eateries and repair shops and dry cleaners that had at one time lined Main Street. Cole's memories, from when he was a kid, were of a neighborhood that had become run-down and despondent, its dignity tattered. Now, however, new paint and siding gleamed on once-shabby houses, while postage-stamp yards that had gone to dirt boasted bright green grass and clumps of vibrant flowers, the occasional, optimistic sapling protectively tethered to the ground.

Hope for the future planted in what had been there all along—

"So Father Bill tells me," Bree said quietly beside him, "an 'anonymous' donor gave the church a nice chunk of change towards the roof repair."

"Oh, yeah?"

"Mmm-hmm. Along with a fancy-schmancy new computer for the office." Her eyes slid to his. "I don't suppose you know anything about that, do you?"

"Can't say that I do," he said, chuckling at her soft groan. Then she sighed.

"You're a good man, Cole Rayburn."

"I never said—"

"Why?"

"Why do I think the past is worth preserving?"

A beat passed before she said, "Sure."

He answered very carefully. Not to mention deliberately. "It isn't always, of course. Sometimes it really is best to gut the whole thing and start over. Especially if it no longer serves a viable purpose. But if it does..." He glanced at her as they walked. "As long as the foundation's solid, anything can be restored. Rebuilt, even."

He saw her forehead knot for a moment before she said, very softly, "So what's Wes into? Sports? Cars? Video games, I assume?" Not what he expected. When he frowned down at her, she chuckled. "Hoping to avoid conversational dead space if we're gonna be stuck in a booth together."

Cole's heart knocked against his rib cage. Was this in response to what he'd said? Or simply Bree being Bree? In any case, she was showing more interest in Wes's preferences than his mother had, ever... Who for the past however many years had asked Cole what she should get the kids for their birthdays and Christmas. And she'd *lived* with them, for God's sake.

"Basketball," he said, and she nodded.

"Right—"

"And filmmaking."

"Really?"

"Huge Spielberg fan. Has been since he was...ten?"

"Good Lord. He's more of a nerd than you were. You must be so proud."

Cole laughed. "He makes these quirky little videos with his phone...blows my mind. And here we are..."

"Wow," Bree said, as they all pushed through the glass door, ringing the overhead bell. "And I thought your parents' place was stuck in time."

The woman spoke the truth. Antonio's hadn't changed a whole lot in twenty years, although Cole was guessing the fake leather booths had been reupholstered at least once since then. And the menu prices were higher. But damned if Connie, the same waitress who used to serve them as kids, didn't take their orders, her hair just as black, her bosom just as…bosomy. And her Jersey-inflected voice every bit as smoke-snarled as Cole remembered.

She barked out their orders toward the guy behind the counter—shakes for him and Sabrina, sundaes for the kids—then looked back, dark eyes narrowed under penciled-on brows. "You look familiar," she said to Sabrina. "You been here before?"

"Years ago," she said, smiling. "When we were teenagers. We used to come in with a tall redhead?"

"Yeah, yeah…I remember now. Knew I wasn't imagining things. You're as cute as ever, doll. I mean that." Then her gaze swung to Cole. "But holy cow…you, I wouldn't've recognized. And I mean that in a good way," she said with a throaty chuckle as she laid a hand on his shoulder. "So these are your kids, huh? Not that I'm surprised. I could've told you then, you two would end up together—"

"No!" Cole said before Wes blew a gasket. "I mean, yes, they're my kids—"

"But not mine," Sabrina said with a glance at Wes before smiling up at Connie again. "I happened to be in town, and we ran into each other. Coincidence," she said with a shrug. "That's all."

"Huh," Connie said, squinting once more. Although that might've been the false eyelashes. "Well, whatever—it's good to see you guys again. And we'll get that order right out to you."

Coincidence, Cole thought, as he watched Sabrina watching Brooke, Sabrina's mouth curved in a soft smile as his daughter prattled on about the dance class she was taking twice a week. Funny how the term had come to mean a random occurrence, something that happened purely by chance, when its root didn't necessarily have the same connotation.

Because was Bree's reappearance in his life really only

random? Or did some higher intelligence have a hand in aligning events and circumstances to bring them together?

Intriguing thought, that.

Connie brought them their treats. The kids dug into their sundaes, and Bree plunked her straw into her chocolate shake, her cheeks sinking in as she sucked up her first, long pull. Cole tried not to notice—or at least, react—but then her eyes practically rolled back in her head, and he thought…things he had no right to be thinking in public. Especially sitting with his kids.

"You know," she said to the table at large, "of all the milk shakes I've had in my life—which must number in the thousands by now—this is still one of the best."

"I could've told you that, doll," Connie said from two tables over. "But thanks."

Bree gave the waitress a thumbs-up, then said, "So Pop and I got into this argument about what's the best Spielberg movie." Beside him, Cole felt Wes jerk to attention. "He says *Schindler's List*. But I kind of have a soft spot for *Close Encounters*."

"What about *Jurassic Park*?"

Bree grinned at the boy. "I watched that so much I wore out the tape."

"The…tape?"

She sighed. "And now I feel about a thousand years old. But the first time was in the movie theater, with Mom and Pop and everybody else. Including this dude," she said, pointing at Cole. "We were—" her brow puckered "—thirteen? It was shortly after we met. Anyway, he was at the house, and we were going, so he got dragged along with the herd."

"So it wasn't, like, a date?"

"Again. Thirteen. And there was a crowd. There also might've been, as I recall, some clandestine popcorn throwing."

"And thank you for putting ideas into my children's heads," Cole said, and Brooke giggled.

"Hey. You started it."

"I did not!"

"Oh, yes you did! Kelly was sitting between us, and you were trying to get my attention—it was right before the tyrannosaurus got the dude sitting on the john, and I was frozen—so you tossed popcorn at my head. And I was furious because you got grease in my hair!"

By this time the kids were laughing so hard they couldn't even eat their ice cream. Including Mr. Grumpy. "Oh, and like you didn't throw it back," Cole said, grinning. Grateful. "And then a piece went down the front of Kelly's top, and she shrieked, and everybody around us got mad, and your father made us change seats so we weren't next to each other."

Sabrina grinned. "God, we were *awful*."

"Don't listen to her, guys," Cole muttered, which only got them laughing harder.

"Yeah. Good times," Bree said softly, wistfully, and Cole wanted to kiss her so badly his mouth actually tingled.

Wanted *her* so badly everything else tingled. Because that thing he'd said, at the wedding? About never letting anyone else get to him like she had when they were kids?

Anyone *else*, maybe. This woman, however…

Afterward, they walked back to their cars, parked on opposite sides of the church parking lot. It was full dark by now, the evening humidity like a soft cloak. A sweetly pungent breeze swept up from the river, laced with the sounds of crickets, the distant thrum of highway traffic, the kids' good-natured arguing as they again walked ahead of them.

"That was fun," he said, and Bree chuckled.

"Yeah. It was. Thanks for asking me."

She stumbled slightly, bumping into him. He caught her, then slipped his hand around hers.

And this time, she didn't even try to pull away.

She'd forgotten how lovely it felt to hold hands. The giddiness the simple touch provoked, starting low in her stomach before shunting with breakneck speed through the rest of her body, making every skin cell hum with anticipation. And yet, oddly, also wrapping her in a deep calm, that she was safe—

"They'll see," she said.

"No, they won't. Too dark."

—a realization that should have kicked the calm into the next state, boy. Except it felt too good to fight.

Friends. That's all...

Chad hadn't liked to hold hands. Not in public, anyway. Not even after they'd slept together. Not that they'd ever discussed it, but her guess was that he saw hand-holding as juvenile. Undignified. Never mind the ancient couples they'd see toddling down the city streets, unashamed to display their affection to all and sundry—

So the jerk wasn't right for you. Moving on...

Yeah. About that.

Really, she should let go of Cole's hand. Giddiness and such aside. Because she did like it and it did make her feel calm and cared about, all of which were so wrong for her right now.

And even more wrong for Cole—

"Go on ahead to the car," he said to the kids. "I'll catch up in a second."

—not to mention those two.

Cole dropped her hand when they reached her car, and she immediately missed his touch. His warmth. Not to mention a strength she now realized had always been part of who he was, even if buried under a gazillion layers of dorkiness and *Star Wars* T-shirts.

Smiling, she turned around, swallowing at the intense expression on his face in the graying light. Funny to think they'd been nearly the same height until their sophomore year of high school.

"Well," she said. "Thanks again."

"No problem."

She could tell he wanted to kiss her. Thank goodness for the kids, then, because, boy-howdy, did she want to kiss him back. Neediness was such a bitch—

Pop's ringtone salsa'd from her purse. Holding up a finger to stop Cole from leaving, she dug it out and answered.

"What's up?"

"You ready for this? I sold the house."

"What? When?"

"About ten minutes ago."

"But…wait. How? The first open house isn't even until Sunday…"

A minute later, still staring stupidly at her phone, her father's news buzzed incoherently inside her brain.

"Bree? Is everything okay?"

"Pop sold the house," she said, the words rushing out. "Cash offer. Young couple. They want…they want to take possession ASAP. In other words…" Her throat clogged. "In a week I'm homeless—"

Too late, she realized what she'd walked right into.

"And maybe now," he said quietly, "would be a good time to tell me the whole truth. About why you're here. Because this isn't only about your *emotional* recuperation, is it?"

Her mouth pulled tight. "I moved in with Chad when we got engaged, more than a year ago. Since he was paying for the apartment—and everything else—I insisted on footing most of the bill for the wedding. A lot of the deposits weren't refundable. So when we broke up…" She shrugged. "I still have some savings, but not enough for the up-front fees on a new place, since I'd let mine go. Obviously."

Cole's brow knotted. "And he didn't offer to reimburse you?"

"Yeah, well….seems Chad was having a few cash-flow problems himself."

"Which you didn't know."

"Nope."

His gaze was so intense she shivered. "You could have asked me for the money."

Not one word about how imprudent she'd been. How careless and trusting and naive. Her eyes burned. "My problem to solve, Cole. No one else's. Especially not yours."

He shook his head, muttering something she was just as glad she couldn't make out. "Fine. But you're not homeless—"

From twenty feet away, Wes called to him, asking what was going on.

Good question.

"—because the guest suite over the garage? It's yours."

"What? Cole, no, I couldn't, I'll bunk with…"

Yeah. Who? And where? On Matt's lumpy sofa? With Tyler and Laurel, who were still in honeymoon phase?

She looked up at Cole, whose smile even in the dark took her heart rate to the next level. Dammit.

"But the kids—"

"Will deal. Go home. We'll talk later."

Somehow, she got behind the wheel—nothing like shaking knees to make that little maneuver awkward as hell— jumping a little when Cole tapped his palm on the car's hood and walked away.

She told herself she was only staring at his butt as it— and he—retreated, but she knew she was lying. Sighing, she started the car, drove out of the lot, thinking anytime the universe wanted to stop messing with her, she'd be good.

"What the heck is *wrong* with you?"

About to throw the ball for the dogs for the eight millionth time, Wesley flinched at the sound of his sister's voice. Obviously, the girl who used to be scared of basically everything was gone. He half wished she'd come back.

Another change, he thought, throwing the tennis ball so hard it bounced off the back wall, making all three dogs trip over each other trying to get it. Pretty much the way his brain felt these days.

"Cripes, Brooke, keep your voice down. Dad's got the windows open up there." He jerked his head toward the bedroom over the garage, where Dad was cleaning or whatever. For Sabrina.

"He's vacuuming, he can't hear anything." His sister crossed her arms over her stomach. "Is this about Sabrina coming to stay here?"

Moe growled as Wes tugged the slobbery ball out of the dog's mouth, galloping off with his brothers when it sailed across the yard again. "Maybe."

"You are such an idiot."

Wes turned on her. "*I'm* the idiot? She's not going to be here forever, Brooke. And even if she was..." His throat going all tight, he squatted to wrestle the ball away from Curly this time.

"I know what she said. I also know..." His sister glanced up at the open window, then lowered her voice. "I know Dad likes her. A lot. And why wouldn't he? She's like the coolest person ever. So maybe he can change her mind?" At his eye roll, she said, "Oh, come on, Wes—you heard them, at the diner. The way they joke with each other and stuff. It was *fun*. And it felt good. And you can't tell me it didn't. So, wouldn't it be great, if they got together—"

"For heaven's sake, Brooke—*grow up*."

It was a horrible thing to say, and he knew it. However, instead of telling him to stop treating her like a baby, like usual, all she did was glare at him for a second before she spun around and stomped back inside. Leaving Wes feeling even angrier than before. Mostly because Brooke was right. About all of it.

Including the part about Sabrina being cool.

And that scared him so much it hurt to breathe.

Chapter Eleven

"There's no one in New York you could stay with?"

It was the first thing Matt had said since leaving Pop's house. Making the five-block drive the longest trip, ever.

"My assistant offered, but (*a*) she's twenty-two, and (*b*) she lives in a studio. Way out near JFK. Takes less time to get from *here* to Thirty-Fourth Street than from her place."

Pulling into Cole's driveway, Matt glowered at the house. As if he was taking her to prison. Or a psychiatric facility. And he didn't know the half of it. And, God willing, never would. Granted, they were talking nearly twenty years ago, but some things you don't want your überprotective brother to know.

"It's perfectly safe, Matty. Especially with the kids there—"

"What makes you think I'm worried about you, numbskull? Cole's the one with the problem here. Not you—"

Again. Ignorance was bliss.

"—because far as I can tell? The dude's as crazy about you as ever. So watch it, okay?"

"You do remember he dumped me, right?"

"And whatever the reason was for that? I'm guessing he got over it." He paused. "I'm also guessing you did."

"Maybe because, I don't know—that was a million years ago? However, have no fear, big guy. Since I'm not about to jump into another relationship."

"And I'm supposed to believe that?"

Her face heated. Since her history wasn't exactly a secret. "Not this time, okay? And, yeah, I know I've said that before, but…" Her hand fisted around her purse straps. "I'm not going to do anything stupid. Especially since there's kids involved. And anyway, Cole isn't looking for anything, either. No matter what you think you see."

Or, more to the point, what *she* saw. Felt.

Knew.

Her brother touched her knee. "Just be careful, okay? The two of you, you're like nitro and glycerin right now. Put you together and…" He made a one-handed exploding gesture, complete with sound effect.

Rolling her eyes, Sabrina got out of the car and opened the back door. "And you, brother dear," she said, grabbing her suitcase and carry-on, then her purse and tote bag, "have been watching way too much reality TV." She slammed shut the door and yanked up the suitcase's handle, then leaned over beside the open passenger-side window. "But thanks for caring, okay?"

Shaking his head, her brother backed out of the drive as Cole came through the front door—barefoot, in shorts and a T-shirt—meeting her halfway to take the suitcase and carry-on from her. He looked a little damp, as if he'd been working out, maybe. T-shirt clinging to pecs, hair curlier than usual. And she thought, *Safe? Like hell.*

"Matt giving you a hard time?"

"It's what he does," she muttered as she followed Cole inside, and three very excited doggies rushed her, smushing their little flat noses into her calves. She bent over to give them all some loving, thinking, *Now what?*

"Kids are at my sister's," Cole said in an odd voice, as though he wasn't quite sure what came next, either. "Um... the bed's made up in the guest suite, there's clean towels in the bath. It's pretty small, though."

"That's okay, so am I," she said, and he smiled.

"I thought maybe pizza for dinner?" He paused. "Home-made."

"Dude. Impressive."

He chuckled. "How's your dad doing?"

"Pretty well, surprisingly, considering how fast it happened. But to tell you the truth, he seems more at peace than I've seen him in a long time. Going with the flow. Which we all know is not his strong suit. And his apartment's really nice. One of the larger units, gorgeous view of the grounds. And he can take his meals in the dining room or cook his own, a-and..."

Damn it. She was not going to cry. Okay, she was. But she certainly wasn't going to admit how good it felt to find herself in Cole's arms, breathing in his scent, feeling his warmth. *His* warmth, *his* scent, *his* arms...

He steered her toward the living room's dusty blue-velvet sofa, all three dogs milling around their feet, worried. One jumped into her lap when they sat; she pulled the sturdy little pooch against her stomach as Cole did the same to her.

"It's c-crazy...I haven't lived in that house in years. And yet, when I walked away today and realized I'd never see inside again, never see my room, or the backyard, or any of it..."

With that, the tears came. Not an ugly cry—thank God— but a slow, steady release of emotion she could no longer restrain. Or deny.

Cole turned and handed her the tissue box. She yanked one out, clutching it after she blew, sending the startled dog scrambling off her lap. "I remember how scared I was, when Matt and I first arrived. How these two people we'd never seen before immediately made us feel like we belonged. How loud and crazy it could get, with all the kids and dogs..." She looked at Cole. "And then you guys. You and Kelly, I mean... I'm sorry," she said on a shaky breath. "I'm not making a whole lot of sense..."

"It was your *home*, honey," Cole murmured, gently brushing her hair off her temple. "Your childhood. So you're allowed to grieve, yo."

She gave a wobbly laugh, then sighed. "I can't even imagine what Pop is going through right now."

"Wanna invite him for dinner? The kids would love it."

"That's sweet, but Matt and Kelly already have that covered. For tonight, anyway. But thanks." Blowing her nose again, she stood, tugging down her top. "Well. Guess I should see about making my nest. And I'm sure you have things to do. I don't want to disrupt your alone time. Which must be more precious to you than ever, with the kids—"

"Who I miss like crazy when they're not around," he said with a soft smile as he got to his feet, as well. "Because they're part of my bubble." His eyes darkened. "Same as you were, when we were kids. And you know what? Nothing's changed on that score—"

The kids burst through the front door, arguing at the top of their lungs about something or other. Spotting Sabrina, Brooke squealed and ran over to give her a hug. Wes, however, only gave her a passing glance before heading down the hall.

"What do you want on your pizza?" Cole called after him.

"Do whatever you want," the boy lobbed back, followed by his door slamming shut.

Sabrina guessed they weren't talking about pizza anymore.

Cole didn't wait for Wes to acknowledge his rap on the kid's door before pushing it open, earning him a thunderous look and an affronted, "What the *heck,* Dad? You're not supposed to come in unless I say it's okay!"

Cole slipped his hands into his pants pockets. "Why not?"

Wes's forehead knotted. "Because it's *rude*?"

"So let me get this straight—it's not okay for me to open your door without your permission, but it is for you to blow off our guest. Is that how it goes?"

The rims of the kid's ears turned bright red. One of many traits he'd inherited from Cole. Poor guy.

"I'm—"

"Save it," Cole said. "And, no, I'm not going to ask you to apologize—"

Dark brows crashed together. "You're…not?"

"No. Because an insincere apology would be even worse." Now the blush flooded the boy's cheeks. "Not to mention Sabrina would see straight through it. But let's get something straight, right now—I get that you're still upset about what happened with your mom. That everything already feels unsettled without bringing somebody else into the house. So I'm not saying your feelings are entirely unjustified. But taking those feelings out on that somebody else—a somebody else who was not only my best friend when we were kids, but who's going through some pretty crappy times of her own right now—is *not* justified. *Ever.* You don't have to like her. You don't even have to like that she's here. But you will be polite and treat Sabrina with the same respect you'd want for yourself. Is that clear?"

Nostrils flared, Wes looked away, breathing heavily. But after a moment, he nodded. Good enough.

Because God knew Cole couldn't fix much in this world—his world, at least—but no way was his own kid going to act like a jerk.

"Okay, then. I'll let you know when dinner's ready. And, yes, I expect you to join us. No holing up in here. Got it?"

"How long is she staying?"

"As long as she needs to," Cole said quietly, then left the room, not bothering to shut the door behind him.

The soft laughter coming from the kitchen was such a stark contrast to the tension and misery in his son's room, it took Cole a moment to readjust, like coming out into the light from a cave. Bree and his daughter had already assembled two pizzas, one cheese and one with apparently everything they could find in the fridge. Smiling, Sabrina looked up when he came in, even as questions shimmered in those deep, dark eyes. Brooke's phone rang; after she left to take the call, Bree whispered, "He okay?" her genuine concern twisting Cole up inside.

"I'm sure he doesn't think so." He plucked several more slices of pepperoni out of the package, added them to the pie. "We like a freakish amount of pepperoni."

"Yeah? Me, too." Then Bree sighed. "Listen, if my being here is going to cause that much turmoil, there's always Matt's sofa—"

"For Wes, maybe. Not you."

Her laugh was soft. But sad, Cole thought. Couldn't blame her for that.

"Are *you* okay?"

"Not really, no," she sighed out. "I will be, of course. And I'm grateful for…this. Truly. But…" Shaking her head, she placed the last few black olive slices on the pizza, then crossed her arms, frowning at it.

"Not how you saw your life at this point?"

"I at least thought I'd have my own home by now." A short laugh pushed from her chest. "Someplace I could paint the walls whatever the hell color I wanted."

"Even hot pink?"

She grinned. "Maybe."

Cole slipped the pizzas in the oven, then turned back around, leaning his butt against the counter edge. "In New York, I take it?"

"You bet. Probably not Manhattan, though. Too expensive. But Brooklyn, maybe." Her smile softened. "A brown-stone."

He smiled back. "On a tree-lined street?"

"What else?"

Wes suddenly appeared outside the kitchen, right behind Bree, his hands shoved in his pockets. "Hey, buddy," he said as she twisted to face the boy. "What's up?"

Wes's gaze darted from Cole to Bree, then back to Cole. "Dinner ready yet?"

"Ten minutes."

The boy nodded, then hauled in a breath big enough to inflate a Macy's Parade balloon before looking back at Bree. "I'm sorry I was rude earlier, Sabrina. And I'm not just saying that, I mean it. Because Dad said you'd know if I was faking it."

Cole glanced over, catching Bree's desperate attempt to keep a straight face, but the expression in her eyes…oh, man.

"Your dad speaks the truth," she said, humor glinting in those eyes. Humor, and patience, and such deep, sweet understanding it was everything Cole could do not to lay one on her right there. Then she uncrossed her arms, reaching out to gently squeeze Wes's shoulder. "But it's okay, honey. No hard feelings." Then she crossed her arms again, giving him a soft smile. "So. We're okay?"

"Yeah, I guess," Wes said with a glance at Cole.

Maybe not wholesale acceptance, exactly, but a start. And he'd take it. Because Cole knew there was no winning over Bree until Bree won over his kids.

He could only pray that happened before the clock ran out.

"Wondered where you'd gotten to."

And wasn't it telling that, despite the ninety-degree temperature outside, a chill scampered up Sabrina's back at the sound of Cole's voice. With her legs stretched out in front of her on the chaise, she smiled.

"One thing I've never been able to do in New York. Sit outside at night like this. Listen to the crickets."

She sensed more than saw him sit in the chair beside her. "No stoops? No fire escapes?"

"No crickets. None that I could hear over the traffic noise, anyway."

"So Jersey does have its pluses."

"Not that you'll ever get me to admit that," she said, smiling, and he snorted.

He had no idea, of course, that—because, open door and small house—she'd overheard his conversation with Wes earlier. Not all of it, but enough. Enough to feel a tingle of almost painful pleasure that he'd stood up for her. Even though she wasn't staying.

Of course, there was the possibility that his taking his son to task had less to do with her and more to do with Cole being the kind of father who wasn't going to let his kid get away with crap.

The kind of dad Pop had been. Still was.

The kind of man...

She lifted her glass of iced tea to her lips, stopping the thought. The fantasy.

The dream.

"Kids in bed?" she said.

"Probably. Di took them swimming. That always conks them out early." She felt him look at her in the dark. As in, literally *felt*, as though his gaze was actually heated. Considering the temperature, no easy feat. She shuddered again, and things...perked. "Great pizza, by the way," he said.

She chuckled. "The parts were already there. All I did was put it all together. And you added the extra pepperoni, if you recall."

"True."

She could hear the smile in his voice. Now she looked

over, although she couldn't see much in the dark. Down by the wall, dogs snuffled. "You sound…at peace."

"Do I?" He blew out a breath. "I guess I am, at the moment. Wanna know why?"

No. "Sure."

"The same reason I used to when we were kids. When we'd hang out." He extended his long, muscled legs, lacing his hands behind his head. "Only time I did feel that way. When I was with you." At her silence, he said, "Have I spooked you?"

Hell, yes. "No, not at all. I'm glad…well. Just that. I'm glad."

"As you damn well should be."

Sabrina smiled, wondering how she could feel so comfortable with someone who made her so *un*comfortable. Who made her squirmy and itchy and fluttery and achy. Oh, dear God, achy. Feelings she'd felt before, alas. Which always led to Things That Did Not End Well.

Always.

"Have you decided on a school for the kids?"

A moment's beat told her he was parsing the subject change. "We're on a couple of waiting lists, but if they don't pan out, we could homeschool for a year, if we had to." He softly laughed. "Providing the kids and I don't kill each other."

"There is that." Then she frowned. "A couple of lists? So…private school, then?"

"Or charter. Whatever's best for them. We have options."

"Not a whole lot in Maple River."

"Like I said…" Now when he turned toward her, she saw the flash of his smile. "Options."

And why that single word made the hair stand up on the back of her neck, she had no idea.

A few days later, Cole was in the kitchen preparing dinner—with the usual entourage of panting, hopeful pugs—when he heard the front door open, the telltale clunk of Bree's tote bag hitting the tiled entryway floor and Brooke's excited chatter as she regaled the poor woman with every single detail of her day. A minute later, a chuckling Bree stuck her head into the kitchen, the only person he knew who could make worn-out look sexy.

"God, that smells good."

Or could make such an ordinary comment *sound* sexy.

"Spaghetti. Garlic bread. Not exactly gourmet." He frowned at the shopping bag dangling from her hand. "Saks?"

"What shopping bag?" she said, mischief dancing in her eyes. "And spaghetti sounds amazing. Going to change, these shoes are killing me."

"Can I come with?" his daughter asked.

"Of course." She rattled the bag. "Who do you think this is for?"

Cole sighed. "Bree…"

"Summer clearance, dirt cheap," she said, her grin infectious as she took his beaming daughter by the hand. "I swear."

"Dinner's in about a half hour, when Wes gets home from Keenan's."

"Great. I'm starving."

After they left, though, Cole's own smile faded. In the past three days she'd had four appointments, two of which were new referrals from current clients. Meaning—if her bright-eyed expression when she'd told Cole the news was any indication—she'd soon have the funds she needed to start the apartment search. In the city. Which also meant his window of opportunity was rapidly closing.

Although to accomplish what, exactly, he'd yet to figure out. Since even if by some miracle they worked out whatever the issues were between them, no way would Bree ever move back to Maple River. And Cole still couldn't see himself living in New York. Not without a steady supply of happy pills, anyway.

Then there was Wes, who, although living up to his end of the bargain about being respectful to Bree, still wasn't entirely reconciled to her being there. And he knew Bree would never even consider anything more as long as Wes was resistant. Not after what she'd just gone through with her ex's kid.

Sighing heavily, Cole clamped the glass top back on the spaghetti-sauce pot. Sure, they were all getting along okay. More than okay—he wondered if Bree even realized how easily she fit into their lives, sharing meals and chores, even agreeing on what movies or TV shows to watch. On the surface, things were hunky-dory, despite the occasional worried sideways glance, as if she was wondering when he was going to pounce.

Hell, he had no idea what he was doing. How to level up. Since gold coins or magic flowers or special hammers weren't magically appearing to help him out.

He turned when Brooke reappeared, wearing a conglomeration of clothing he couldn't have described if his life had depended on it. But he definitely saw the short shorts—or at least, they seemed pretty damned short to him—which made her legs look…long.

Legs which ended in a pair of the ugliest, clunkiest shoes he'd ever seen.

If he lived to be a thousand, he'd never understand women's fashion.

"Bree's taking a shower. Want me to make a salad?" she asked, clomping to the fridge. Like a giraffe in Frankenstein shoes.

"Sure, that'd be great," Cole said, grabbing the loaf of French bread to slice as Brooke chattered from the other side of the kitchen. And his chest ached, at how much she'd changed over the past few weeks.

Because of Bree, who'd worked the same wonders with

Brooke as she had with him. A gift she didn't even know she possessed, he thought as the woman herself appeared, smelling of body wash and shampoo and wearing shorts and a tank top that left far less to the imagination—Cole's, anyway—than she probably realized, her hair hanging in curvy ropes around her shoulders. He allowed himself a second's torturous kick to the gut before turning back to the bread.

She came around to sit on the other side of the breakfast bar, her hands folded in front of her. And apparently unaware that a drop of water from her wet hair was trickling into her cleavage. Slowly. Glistening...ly.

Cole reminded himself that he was a dad. A dad on duty. In charge of impressionable young humans.

"Thanks for the clothes," he muttered, cutting off a chunk of butter to melt for the bread.

"Couldn't pass them up, not at that price. Plus, I knew how cute they'd be on the kid," she said, grinning at Brooke behind him. But when her gaze glanced off his, he saw the caution. The doubt.

Which is when it hit him. Like a freaking sledgehammer between the eyes.

Why would she be cautious if she *didn't* feel anything?

"Crap!"

He jerked around at his daughter's cry, reaching her a split second before Bree did. Trembling, Brooke was holding her hand.

Her profusely bleeding hand.

Out of nowhere, paper towels appeared, which he quickly and tightly wrapped around the wound before yanking the poor kid's hand above her head.

"I don't know what h-happened, I was being so careful—"

"It's okay, sweetie," he whispered, touching his forehead to hers before stealing a glance at Bree, calmly cleaning up the...mess.

"Hey," she said, "you didn't get blood on your new clothes, did you?"

That got a shaky chuckle. "I d-don't think so."

"So, silver lining, right?"

That got another little laugh before Cole carefully lowered his little girl's hand and even more carefully peeled away the blood-soaked towel. The cut was deep enough to make his heart jitter, but the bleeding had pretty much stopped, thank God. Bree gave the counter one last swipe with a paper towel, then looked over.

"What do you think?" Cole asked. "Stitches?"

"Definitely—"

"Dad! No!"

"Go on, get her to Urgent Care," Bree said. "I'll hold down the fort here. Hey, hey, hey…" At Brooke's whimpering, Bree cupped the back of the girl's head. "You see this?" She lifted up her shirt to show a three-inch scar on her waist. "You don't even want to know how I got this, trust me. And my poor father—I swear, he turned green. Twelve stitches." She lowered her shirt. "But by the next day it was no big deal. You're gonna be fine, cookie, I promise." She smiled. "And maybe I'll bake something while you're gone."

"Wh-what?"

"Have no idea, depends on what we've got. So get outta here," she said, kissing Brooke on top of her head, then rewrapping the kid's hand in a clean paper towel. "Keep holding the towel tight, like that. Okay?"

Her lower lip quivering as she nodded, Brooke started for the living room as Cole grabbed his keys from a hook by the patio door.

"Thanks," he said softly, and Bree shrugged.

"No big deal."

"Like hell," he said, slipping his hand around her neck, underneath her still wet hair, and quickly—but firmly—pressing his mouth to hers.

"Yeah. That," he said to her startled expression, then booked it the hell out of there, thinking, *Game on, honey*.

Clearly, her staying here was a mistake.

Ya think?

A couple more jobs, Sabrina thought, her eyes burning as she slammed baking pans and such onto the counter, and she'd have enough to at least start looking for a place. Maybe in Washington Heights. Or Jackson Heights, she wasn't picky.

The past few days had been hell. Not in the way most people would use the word, but hell nonetheless. Because— Wes's grumpiness aside—she fit in too damn well with this family. Like she…belonged.

A thought that beckoned and teased, even as it settled like a lead weight in her stomach. Because to accept the promise, only to have it ripped away from her—again— would kill her.

Worse, though, was what it would do to these kids. Brooke, anyway.

And Cole. Oh, hell…the look in his eyes, after he'd kissed her…

She closed her own against the pain. Only to snap them open again when she heard the front door open.

"Dad?"

"In here, Wes," Sabrina called back, quickly swiping a napkin under her eyes.

Frowning, the boy appeared on the other side of the breakfast bar. "Where's Dad?"

"Your sister had an accident—nothing too serious, she'll be fine—but he had to take her to Urgent Care for stitches."

"Stitches?"

"Paring knife. Cut hand. And I repeat, she'll be fine. Um…if you're hungry I can put on the pasta, we can eat whenever. Or we can wait—your dad texted me a few minutes ago, they were already in with the doctor. So it shouldn't be too long."

"I'll wait. Thanks." The boy crossed his arms, his hands stuffed in his armpits as he glowered at the things on the counter. "What are you doing?"

"Making an applesauce cake. Thought it'd be good with vanilla ice cream after dinner. While it's still warm. The cake, I mean. Oh…and I got you something on the way home after work. It's on the coffee table in the living room."

"What?"

"You'll have to go see, won't you?"

The boy disappeared, returning a minute later with the book, a hundred-pound tome on the history of filmmaking.

"And if nothing else," Sabrina said, not looking at him as she poured applesauce into the cake batter, "you can use it to build up your abs."

The sound he made was more snort than laugh. "Okay, if this is you trying to, like, pay me to like you…"

"Hey. Saw the book, thought of you, bought it. End of story. Deal. Or don't." She spooned the batter into a greased pan, shrugged. "Up to you."

At his silence, she looked up, nearly crumpling at his conflicted expression. Which vanished so quickly she almost thought she'd imagined it.

"So, when are you going back to New York?" he asked, thunking the book on to the bar and cracking it open, then slowly turning the pages.

"Can't wait to get rid of me, huh?"

"That's not—" The book slammed closed. "It's not horrible, having you here, okay? I mean…" He nodded toward the pan, and Sabrina smiled, then slipped the pan into the hot oven. "It's…I don't know. I can't always explain what I feel. And I know it seems like I hate you and stuff, but—" he blinked "—I don't."

Ah, hell. Twist her heart inside out, why not?

Sabrina leaned on the counter, her hands folded in front

of her. "I think what you hate is feeling like everything's turned upside down."

"Yeah, maybe." Big, gray eyes lifted to hers. "What you said, at the wedding? Is that still true?"

Slowly, she nodded, even as her eyes stung. "Pretty much. It's just…" She looked at her hands for a moment, then back at Wes. "It's never a good idea to start something new when you've still got junk to deal with from the past. Things get too…mixed-up."

"But you like my dad."

"I like all of you guys—"

"Not what I asked."

"I know. But that's my answer."

His gaze tangled with hers for several seconds before he pushed himself off the bar stool. "Thanks again for the book," he mumbled, hauling it into his arms before trudging away.

Yeah, Sabrina thought, giving the spaghetti sauce another stir. The sooner she made her escape, the better. Because one broken heart was bad enough.

Four, however…not happening.

If it wasn't already too late.

Chapter Twelve

The next morning, Cole was up before the kids, putting on coffee when his phone dinged.

Unexpected appointment, the text read. Didn't want to wake you guys. Will be in the city most of the day. Don't hold dinner, I'll get something here.

Straightforward enough. No lines to read between, really. And yet dread shuddered through him, an apprehension brought on by Bree's strangeness the night before, after he and Brooke got back from Urgent Care and they all had dinner and then watched a movie—his daughter's pick, since she was the one with the boo-boo. And that whole time, even though Bree had laughed and joked with the kids as usual, even as he'd sensed she and Wes had at least inched closer, he could tell something was off.

More off, anyway.

He was guessing the kiss had something to do with that. A kiss that had clearly shocked her, yes, but hadn't disgusted her. Because if it had...well. This was Bree they were talking about. He'd seen her smack the living day-lights out of some dude who'd for whatever reason felt en-titled to make a grab at her. And that was twenty years ago. He highly doubted anything had changed on that score, that she'd have no trouble letting a guy know when he'd crossed a line.

He also doubted he'd imagined how her pupils had di-lated. The flush that had swept across her chest, up her neck, to bloom in her cheeks. Yeah, he knew how things worked now.

Except how to make things work with her.

And time was running out.

At least the day passed uneventfully enough. As Bree had predicted, his daughter seemed barely aware of her stiches—only two, and in a spot that wouldn't see much action, thank God—and one of the kids from church had taken Wes over there to shoot hoops for the afternoon. Now, edging toward ten, Cole was in the living room watching *Breaking Bad* for the third time when, as one, the dogs lifted their heads at the sound of a car pulling into the driveway, then leaped to their feet and pranced toward the door. Cole stood as well, his hands rammed in his pockets, his heart knocking against his ribs.

"Hey," he said softly when Bree opened the door to a sea of quivering, buff-colored canine love. Wearing one of those straight, sleeveless dresses she apparently had in every color imaginable, her eyes glanced off his as she set her purse on the floor, a habit he'd already grown accus-tomed to.

Her smile seemed shaky. "Hey, yourself. Kids asleep?"

"In their rooms."

"How's Brooke?"

"Resilient. How come you didn't ask me for a ride to the station this morning?"

"Um, the kids?"

"Considering neither of them were up before eleven, they would've been fine for an hour—"

"I saw Chad."

Cole's stomach plunged. "Oh?"

"He—" she looked absolutely miserable "—he returned the ring and gave me the money. To make up for what I'd spent on the wedding."

"And you accepted it."

Her eyes glistened. "He insisted."

"Wow. That was nice of him."

"It was. Especially since it means…"

"You can get your own place now."

"Yeah."

Blood roared in his ears. "Still. You can stay as long as you like, you know. Take your time looking—"

"The commute's making me crazy," she said softly, her eyes giving the lie to her words. "Especially since I'm more booked than ever. S-so I've already contacted an agent I know, one of my clients. She's got several places lined up for me to look at. Tomorrow, actually. And…" He saw her swallow. "And I'm staying with my assistant in the meantime. On her futon, but since it's only for a few days…"

"Wow," Cole pushed out. "When you decide to do something, you don't mess around, do you?"

She blinked. "Hey, you don't dillydally with the New York rental market. You snooze, you lose."

Now he crossed his arms high on his chest, right over the spot where it felt as if someone had poured gasoline on it and tossed in a match. "Is this where I wish you all the best in your future endeavors?"

"Cole, please—"

"Well, screw that," he said, stepping closer, close enough to see a thousand emotions swirling in her dark, wet eyes before he clamped his hands on her shoulders and kissed her again, tasted her, hard enough to show he meant business, softly enough to make her moan…for a second or so before she roughly pulled free.

"*This* is what's not happening," she said, her voice shaking. "Because what would be the fricking point?"

"The point is *us*. All of us, together, as a family—"

"And that's a lovely dream, Cole. Really. But that's all it is—a dream. And whatever the hell happened to all that 'never again' stuff—"

"I lied?"

Several interminable seconds later, she said, "You do realize there's no guarantee it would work?"

"If you need more time—"

"For what? For Brooke and me to get even closer? And who knows, maybe Wes would even finally come around. Only who's to say you don't wake up one day and realize you'd made a mistake—"

"And what makes you think that's going to happen?"

Tears crested in her eyes. "Because it always does, Cole. Always. I don't know why, but it does. And is that a risk you really want to take? With them?" Her throat worked again. "For yourself? And it would kill me…." She shook her head. "So…no. Maybe you're okay with going down roads that lead nowhere, but I'm done. Now if you don't mind, I'm going to bed. Matt's coming really early to pick me up."

"You're not even going to say goodbye to the kids?"

"It's already killing me to leave *you*," she said softly, and his heart jumped. "The kids…I can't."

Tension vibrated between them for several seconds before Cole stepped aside, hands raised, his stomach churning as Sabrina walked past him.

Sighing, he massaged the back of his neck as he let the dogs out back, followed them onto the patio. Oddly enough, he really did understand where she was coming from. After all, he didn't exactly have the greatest relationship track record, either. And God knew he'd spent way too many nights lying in bed and staring up at his ceiling, wondering *why*. On the face of it, her fears were more than justified, and he couldn't, wouldn't, fault her for them. Or for wanting to avoid more pain.

Except giving up…it didn't feel right.

So don't, bonehead.

His heart knocking against his ribs, he dropped onto the edge of the nearest chair, dragging his hands down his face to blow a breath into his cupped palms.

What he was thinking…it was crazy. But you know what? Not any crazier than what he did to pay the bills. And once again, it occurred to him that the best gamers, the ones who were always on top of the leaderboards, were the risk takers, the mavericks…the ones who not only made the most of whatever opportunity popped up on the screen, but who hunted those suckers down like their lives depended on it. That'd been him, once upon a time, back when winning the game was all that mattered.

Only this was no game.

This was his life.

Sabrina had just zipped up her packed suitcase when the light rap on the door made her jump.

And if she had an ounce of sense, she'd ignore it and maybe Cole would think she was already asleep.

With the light on. Right.

Tightening her robe sash, she padded barefoot across the carpet to open the door. Where, yep, stood the man of the hour, hands slugged into his front pockets, all shoulders and pecs and serious silver eyes, and she was a goner.

Not that she hadn't been before.

"Did I wake you?" Cole said, his voice gravelly soft as he let his gaze drift over the flimsy robe, and she couldn't breathe. Or think, really.

She shook her head. "What do you want?"

He reached out to finger her hair, letting his knuckle

skim her cheek, her jaw. She trembled. Dammit. His mouth twitched.

"Guess."

"Fresh out of sugar, sorry."

"Oh, I don't know about that," he said, smiling, as the knuckle wandered, unsteadily, down the side of her neck, across her collarbone. "You gonna smack me?"

"Thinking about it."

He let the backs of his fingers graze her nipple, underneath the silky fabric, so slowly, so…perfectly. There were twinges. Exquisite. Sweet. "Now's your chance."

Yeah. *Smacking* him was not what she wanted to do right now.

"R-rain check," she murmured.

He stilled. "On?"

"I'm not gonna hit you, okay?"

"Then…may I come in?"

"It's your house."

"But it's your space."

"Only until…" She swallowed, then stepped back. "Sure."

He palmed her waist, moved them inside the room. Shut the door behind him. Untied the robe.

Tugged her close.

And her hormones did the Kermit flail. *Yaaaaayyyyy…*

"The kids—"

"Dead to the world," he whispered, his hands hot, gentle, against her bare skin…his breath warm, teasing, against her temple. *Who are you?* she wanted to say. Except she knew exactly who he was.

Who he'd always been.

"Still waiting," he said softly, slipping the robe off her shoulders.

"For?"

"You to say no." Now his lips were on her neck, right…

there… "Because you can, you know," he said, moving north, then south again. "Anytime."

Then he brought their mouths together, his teasing and demanding and generous, all at once, and angels sang. Loudly. And for an amazingly long time.

"You don't play fair," she muttered when the damn things finally shut up. More or less.

"This is true."

Sabrina laughed. She couldn't help it. Even as tears clogged her throat. Then Cole backed up, his forehead pinched.

"Crap. I don't have—"

"I'm on the patch," she said. You know, before the *logical* side of her brain could get a word in over the still-humming angels.

His sigh of obvious relief made her laugh again. Still…

Blinking, she took his face in her hands. "This doesn't change anything—"

"Doesn't it?" he said, before grabbing the hem of his T-shirt, yanking it over his head. She reached for the lamp, to turn it off. Smiling, he clasped her wrist.

"No damn way," he murmured, lowering her to the mattress.

Oh, man, were her nipples happy little campers right now, as Cole tongued and tugged, sucked and stroked and soothed, like nobody was in any rush, here…even as anticipation suffused every molecule with a lovely, languorous heat that only intensified, somehow, when the breeze from the open window caressed her skin. Sure, way at the back of her nonfunctioning brain a shrill little voice whispered, *You're so gonna regret this, pumpkin.* But right now, in this incredibly precious moment, she did. Not. Care.

Feeling hugely Zen and magnanimous, she reached for him, but he grabbed her hand, held it over her head.

"So, what? I don't get to touch, too?"

"Oh, you'll get your chance. When I give the word."

"Jerk."

Chuckling, Cole shifted to one elbow, letting his gaze sweep down, then up, then down again, smiling when she blushed.

"You're getting a kick out of this, aren't you?"

"You have no idea," he said. "Because that first time—"

"Could we please not talk about that?"

"In the dark, in the car…" His eyes met hers again. "I've always wondered if you wanted it like that so you wouldn't have to see—"

"Cole!"

"But that meant I couldn't, either. All those prurient fantasies, dashed. Damned frustrating, that."

"And did it ever occur to you that maybe I wanted it dark so *you* couldn't see?"

He frowned. "I don't—"

"It was my first time, too, remember? And nobody, not even my mother, had seen my breasts before. So I was—" she felt her face warm "—shy."

His brows lifted. "Seriously?"

"Yeah. What? You think I'm making this up?"

Instead of answering, he grinned, then pulled her close again to claim her mouth, his erection pressing against her thigh as he reached between her legs, making her gasp.

And close her eyes.

And moan.

Damn it.

"Not shy now, are we?" he whispered, tormenting, and she made some guttural sound and pressed her hand over his, smiling at his low chuckle in her ear. Not that he needed any guidance, no sir. Dude knew *exactly* what he was doing, clearly attuned to her signals, watching her face—she could feel, even with her eyes shut, that silvery gaze, soft as moonlight on her skin…

"*Now* would be good," she whispered.

Then, a shift of weight, a welcome heaviness as he plunged inside…and several most excellent seconds later her climax roared through her like a damn freight train, *clickity-clack, clickity-clack*…on and on and *on*, holy moly…

Then she felt his shudder, caught his grimace of pleasure morph into a still, sure expression of complete satisfaction before he rolled off her, immediately wrapping her close, kissing her hair, his heartbeat thrumming in her ear.

His laugh was soft. "Think we can safely delete the first time from our memory file," he murmured, and she laughed, too.

Because that's what you did, when the sex was amazing and the person you had sex with was probably the best friend you ever had, or ever will—which was why the sex was amazing. Even though, as you softly fluttered back to earth after a high you'll never forget, you realize exactly how deep is the doo-doo you're in.

Because, sure, she trusted Cole. With her life. And again, amazing sex. Noooo doubt about that, boy. As in, if she died right now, she'd be like, *Go ahead and send me wherever, I've already seen heaven.*

But the worst thing about this? Was that her heart was trying to convince her she was in love. Same as it had soooo many times before.

The difference was, now she knew better than to believe the little stinker. Amazing sex or no. Because she still had no idea what she was doing, what she really wanted. Who she really was.

How to make this stick.

She snuggled closer, her cheek on his chest. "I can't hurt you again, Cole. I won't—"

"Shhh…" He kissed the top of her head. "One step at a time, baby."

One step. Right.

All it took to go right over the edge of the cliff.

* * *

Cole hadn't spent the night, of course. Not that he would have, since it was obvious she needed her space, afterward. Literally as well as figuratively. That much, he could give her. Well, aside from…the other stuff. But he'd also been concerned someone would wake up and wonder where he was. Go looking for him. Not that they had, not since they were toddlers. But with his luck, this would have been the one night they would.

And he would have handled it, somehow. His choice, his consequences. Just as well, however, that he woke up alone this morning, in his own bed.

It was still dark enough, when he stepped into the yard in his pajama bottoms after letting out the dogs, to see the light in the tiny bathroom window overhead. He went back inside, noticed her luggage already by the front door. When on earth had she done that?

He went back to his room, grabbed his phone off the nightstand, texting as he returned to the kitchen:

Do not leave without saying goodbye.

Seconds later:

OK.

Not long after, she appeared at the back door, wearing a short dress and a tiny sweater. Sandals that showed off bright red toenails. And hell, yeah, he got hard. Like he wouldn't?

"What's this?" she said when he handed her a brown paper bag, a thermos.

"Coffee. An egg sandwich. On rye toast, the way you like it."

"Oh, Cole…you didn't have to—"

"Yeah, well, you *didn't have to* last night, either. Deal."

She blushed. Out front, a car pulled up in the drive, the engine's purr drowning out the raucous bird song filtering through the open patio door.

"Um…that'll be Matt—"

"What's going on?" Wes asked, yawning, his hair sticking up every which way like it had when he was a toddler.

"I'm going back to New York, sweetie," Bree said quietly.

"What?" The boy frowned. "When? Now?"

"Yeah," she said, gathering her purse off the counter before reaching up to touch the boy's cheek. "Tell your sister she can call or text me anytime, okay?"

"You're not coming back?"

"My family's still here, so of course I'll visit. But to live?" She shook her head as her phone dinged. "It's Matt," she said, checking the screen before slipping the phone back inside her purse. "I need to go…"

"Let me help you out," Cole said.

"I can manage. And you're not dressed—"

"Like I care what the neighbors think."

Smiling a little, she gave Wes a quick, hard hug, then headed toward the front door, standing on the sidewalk with her arms crossed as Cole silently carted her bags out to Matt's SUV and loaded everything into the back of the car.

"Well," she said after he slammed shut the hatch. "Thanks so much for letting me stay. It was great, getting to know the k-kids…"

She gave her head a sharp shake, then yanked him against her, standing on tiptoe to press her cheek to his and feeling so small and fragile in his arms. So unlike the night before, when she'd been fierce. Uninhibited.

Real and *there* and, for that moment, his.

He held on as long and as tight as he dared, aching that he couldn't kiss her. Not with his son and her brother watching.

But he could whisper, "I wouldn't hurt you, either, baby. Ever," before he let go.

Let *her* go.

Her gaze wrestled with his for a moment before she got in the car, waving to Wes as they backed out of the driveway. Wasn't until they were gone, however, that Cole realized his cheek was wet.

And not from *his* tears.

God.

Wesley spun around from the open front door and stormed back to his room, collapsing into his desk chair so hard it squeaked. A minute later his dad appeared at his doorway. Surprise, surprise.

"Wes—"

"I can't believe you just *stood* there!"

"Keep your voice down. Your sister's still asleep—"

"No, I'm not," Brooke said behind him in the hall in her pajamas, trying to unknot her hair with her fingers. "What's going on?"

"Sabrina's gone, that's what's going on. And Dad didn't even try to stop her."

"What? Dad!"

"Guys! You knew from the beginning she wasn't staying—"

"But she could've changed her mind, right?" Wesley felt like his throat was on fire. "*You* could've changed her mind."

"How? Where she lives, what she does with her life— that's her choice. And anyway—" Dad's eyes narrowed "—I thought you were the one who *didn't* want her around?"

"Yeah," Brooke said, pushing past Dad to plop on Wesley's torn-up bed. "Speaking of changing his mind. What the heck?"

"I didn't think she'd fit, okay?" A dull pain shot through his chest. "That she'd really care about us—"

"Oh, Wesley—"

His eyes shot to his father's. "But it doesn't matter, does it? Because she left, too."

Dad frowned. "Too?"

"Just like Mom."

Behind him, Brooke gasped. "Wait a minute—are you saying you *pretended* you didn't like her? So *you* couldn't get hurt?"

It felt like his face was on fire. "I guess. Maybe."

"Well, that was stupid," his sister said, smacking his shoulder. "Because Sabrina's nothing like Mom! *Nothing!*" Her voice cracked. "You *drove* her away, bozo!"

"It's more complicated than that, guys," Dad said quietly, like he was really tired. "Not that your attitude helped, Wes, but that alone wouldn't have been enough to scare her off. Not our Bree."

The way Dad said her name…

"Except she's not 'ours,' is she?"

Dad looked so hard at Wes he almost shuddered. "Do you want her to be?"

Wes turned away. He didn't know when it happened, when having Sabrina around had started to feel good. Right. Or when he got so scared that it did. But now that she was gone…

"Yes," he whispered, then lifted his head. "Do *you*?"

Dad sighed. "More than you have any idea."

"So," Brooke said, "can you fix this?"

"Truthfully? I don't know." His forehead got all pinchy. "It would probably involve moving to New York, though. Think you guys can hack that?"

Wes and his sister glanced at each other before Brooke said, "But you hate New York."

Dad gave them a funny smile. "Not nearly as much as I love Sabrina."

Weirdly, hearing Dad say that? It didn't make Wes nearly as crazy as he'd thought it would. In fact, just the opposite.

"Then, go for it," he said, and Dad smiled.

And the ache that had been Wes's chest for so long finally eased up a little.

Chapter Thirteen

"So how'd it go?" Frankie shouted the instant Sabrina set foot inside her assistant's basement apartment, vibrating as usual from the booming rock music the girl always had playing. Her head pounding in time with the "music," Sabrina dumped her purse on the floor beside the door, wishing she could ditch the doldrums that had followed her from Jersey a week ago like a pack of stinky dogs.

"Of the three places Leena showed me today," she said, carting her packaged salad into the microscopic apartment's so-called kitchen in search of a fork, "one might work. More than I wanted to pay, though. But at least within reasonable distance of a subway station. And not on the fifth floor. So I should probably take it, huh?"

"Not if it doesn't feel right. Last thing you want is to be locked into a lease on a place that makes you want to kill yourself every time you come home. Believe me, I've been there. And you know you can stay here as long as you need."

With a wan smile, Sabrina sank onto the lumpy futon that doubled as her bed. "Thanks. You really are a sweetheart," she said, prying the top off her plastic container to face yet another meal of limp lettuce and dubious chicken bits. She'd cook if she (*a*) weren't exhausted, and (*b*) felt confident that Frankie's stove—which she'd yet to see the girl use—wouldn't blow up on her.

"Hey, it's nice to have company. Although..." The girl grabbed the carpetbag she used for a purse and her keys. "I've got a date tonight, if that's okay."

"And what am I, your mother? Of course it's okay, why wouldn't it be?"

"Because I feel bad, you being all alone. I know, you don't want to talk about it, but..." Sighing, she dropped the bag. "You know, I don't really need to go out. We could stay in and watch a flick or something—"

"No!" Sabrina said, probably a little too quickly. "Please. Go, have a good time. I'm fine."

"You sure?"

"Absolutely. So get outta here."

That got a skeptical look, but—after tromping over in shoes that were like straitjackets for her feet—Frankie gave Sabrina a hug, then finally left.

Giving up on her so-called dinner, Sabrina grabbed the stereo remote off the coffee table and killed the noise, then let her head fall back on the musty-smelling futon, relishing the silence. The peace. Never before had she appreciated the joy that was being alone as much as she'd learned to this past week.

Although the quiet also brought her thoughts scurrying out of their hiding places like roaches seeking a midnight snack.

Tears, too. Tears over the man she kept reminding herself she needed to get over, because.

Because, because, because...

And how telling was it that, for the life of her, she couldn't finish that sentence?

Oh, God, she missed him. As in, as if she'd left a limb back in Jersey.

And the kids...

Her throat clogged.

Sighing, she got up to dump the gross salad in the trash, deciding—even as pooped as she was—she needed to get out. Take a walk. Mingle with other human beings, even if none of them acknowledged her presence.

It was still light, the air heavy and pearlized—her favorite time of day in the city, especially in the summer. A small crowd surged up from the subway, spilling out on to the street and splintering in a dozen directions, milling around the open-air fruit stands, the florists, the newsstands. She stopped to buy an apple, swiping it across the sleeve of her lightweight top before biting into it, and the sweet tartness, the light and the crowds and the bleat of a taxi horn, made her feel marginally better. Still empty and aching, but better.

Her phone chimed—an incoming text. Her heart stopped when she saw the message.

Find a place yet?

Thinking, *What the hell?* she stepped out of the traffic flow before she got trampled, then texted Cole back.

With shaking hands.

Still working on it.

Where are you?

She frowned at the phone. Typed in the cross streets, then added, In Queens.

Good. DON'T MOVE.

Smirking, she typed back, What if I have to pee?

Two seconds later: Cross your legs.

At which point she launched into the Crazy Lady on the Street Laugh. And, of course, nobody paid her any mind because, hey, New York.

A million years later, a black town car lurched to a stop in front of her, and Cole opened the door and shouted "Get in!" as if they were in some crazy-ass movie. And, as if she was the lead actress in said crazy-ass movie, she did, bumping into him when the car took off again. Of course, she expected him to kiss her—since that would totally go along with the crazy-ass movie thing—but he didn't.

Since, you know, it wasn't.

"What's—"

"You'll see," he said, tossing her a very smug smile that definitely made her girl bits go *Hmm…* Then he reached for her hand, giving it a gentle squeeze, and okay, it felt too nice to object to. Especially since her brain hadn't fully caught up, still hanging back to a half hour before, when she'd been mopey as hell.

When she'd thought she'd never see this man again. Let alone hold hands with him in a hired car zipping through Queens—

Wait.

"Where's your car?"

"At my sister's. With the kids." Then he smiled into her eyes, and that's all she wrote. "Miss me?" he whispered, and she thought, *You should only know.*

"Yes," she pushed out, then faced the window, only her vision was too blurry to see a damn thing.

Not that it mattered, because a second later he'd hauled her into his arms and now he *was* kissing the stuffing out of her, only lifting his mouth long enough to mutter, "Me, too," before resuming the snogfest.

A whole lot of exchanged spit later, they pulled up in front of a sorry-looking brownstone in a very unsorry Brooklyn neighborhood. Quiet—for New York, anyway—tree-lined street, adorable little flower beds at the base of each stalwart little maple, a beautiful old church at the end of the block. The kind of neighborhood she'd fantasized about living in for years. Not as much as she fantasized about the upper East Side, maybe, but short of marrying a rock star or Middle Eastern royalty—neither of which appealed in the slightest—that wasn't gonna happen.

Of course, neither was this, but she was definitely... intrigued.

Especially when it dawned on her, after he'd paid the driver and they were standing on the sidewalk, that there was no for-sale sign in the window.

Sabrina turned to Cole, who was looking at the building with the most self-satisfied grin she'd ever seen on anyone's face. His hair had grown out a little, she noticed, giving him kind of a Roman god vibe—

She nearly choked on her sucked-in breath.

"Holy moly. You bought a house."

"I did indeed."

"In..." She looked back up at it. "Brooklyn."

"It was a toss-up between a school in Cherry Hill and one about six blocks from here." His gaze touched hers, a slight smile curving his mouth. "Since New York's where you were, the kids voted for here."

"Wait. You're telling me I was the deciding factor in where they go to school?"

"Pretty much, yeah. So. Wanna see inside? Although I have to warn you, it needs work."

"I don't—"

"See, we took a vote—although since the outcome was predetermined, it was only a formality—and we decided we weren't ready to give up. On you. On...us. My kids are crazy about you, honey." His eyes softened. "Although not half as much as I am."

She gawked at him, thinking, really, she should run like hell. Because of all those becauses. Which were still lurking, somewhere, ready to pounce. Since it wasn't only the *house* that needed work, here.

"Or just crazy," she muttered, and he laughed.

Then held out his hand.

And God help her, she took it.

"It'd been turned into apartments," Cole said, leading her up the gritty, cocoa-colored steps. With stone planters on either side, begging for geraniums. "Then someone bought it and started converting it back into a single-family home." He unlocked the door, still with most of the original stained glass intact, and the building's history rushed out to embrace her like an excited child. "Except they ran out of money—after gutting all those extra kitchens—and the bank foreclosed."

Jewel-like shards of light danced across the foyer's dusty, gouged wood floor, the paneled walls, and by now Sabrina's heart was in her throat. Especially when she looked up and saw the dingy brass chandelier, then over at the twin rectangles of sunshine spilling across the front room's equally pockmarked floor. She could hear the kids' laughter, reverberating off the high ceiling. Their arguments, too, she thought with a smile—

"Had a crackerjack agent," Cole said. "House came on the market yesterday morning, she showed it to me like five minutes later, I made an offer the bank couldn't refuse right after that. And still came in well under what market value will be, once the reno's finished. The good news is, the previous owners fixed up the basement first, so they'd have someplace to live while they worked on the rest of the house. Brooke's already called dibs on it, for down the road."

"So the kids have seen it?"

"Yesterday. Bedrooms already chosen. Wes in the front, Brooke out back, overlooking the garden."

"Garden?"

Cole grinned. "Go see."

He trailed her to the back of the house, where a small deck off the demolished original kitchen overlooked what had at one time been an adorable little garden. What could be again.

The French doors creaked when she opened them, then stepped out onto worn-smooth wood. Brick walls, she saw. Ivy. A lush maple tree in one corner, masking the apartment building behind. An old but serviceable basketball hoop, mounted on the back wall. Not much space to play, but enough for Wesley to practice his bank shots...

She heard Cole behind her, saying something about six bedrooms and four baths, how the top floor would make a perfect master suite, including a quiet office space for him to work, recharge. A view of the Brooklyn Bridge from the roof...

"So whaddya think?"

Jerking herself out of dreamland, Sabrina went back inside. Heaven help her, was that an original marble fireplace in the dining room? Damn, it was as if he'd pulled the place right out of her head—

"I think...it's beautiful. Or will be, once it's been renovated. I love..." She slowly turned around, taking in the ornamental plaster on the ceiling, the medallion where a gas fixture probably once cast its soft glow over dinner parties and holiday gatherings. "I love how her past is demanding to be remembered. Restored."

"She is a grand old lady, isn't she?" Cole said behind her. "Kind of reminds me of Aunt Lizzie."

Despite the prickling sensation in her eyes, Sabrina smiled. "You and the kids...you're going to be so happy here."

"Only if you're here with us. Although we're still in Jersey for another month, until my parents get back. Until then the basement apartment is yours. If you want it, that is."

Her heartbeat thundered in her ears. And she hadn't even seen the apartment yet. "Do the kids know that's what you're thinking?"

"You kidding? It was their idea. Correction—Wes's idea."

Sabrina whipped around. "But—"

"He was scared, honey. Scared he'd get attached. Only then—"

"I'd leave," she said, then pushed out a dry laugh. "Good Lord—it's like something right out of O. Henry, isn't it?"

Chuckling, Cole tucked her against his chest to lay his cheek in her hair. "You two are a lot more alike than you might think," he said, then shifted to tilt her face to his. "Marry me, honey." He grinned. "You know you want to."

"You are such a turkey," she said. Over the panic.

"A turkey who loves you so much it's like it won't all fit inside me."

"And a poetic turkey, at that."

"It's true. Because you *get* me, Bree. More than anyone I've ever known. More important, you get my kids." He blew a soft laugh through his nose. "Probably more than I do, actually." Then he palmed her cheek, his touch so gentle, so warm, so *there*... "Of course, if you don't love me—"

"I never said that," she whispered, panic be damned, and his gaze softened.

"So you...?"

"Love you, too, okay? Happy now?"

"Uh...yeah?" he said, and she rolled her eyes.

"But it's not a question of whether we love each other—"

"No. It's not a question. It's an irrefutable fact. And remember, I'm the logical one here. So if I say it is, it is."

Her chest aching, Sabrina pulled away to sit on top of a cloth-covered crate or something in the middle of the floor, dropping her face in her hands. A moment later she sensed Cole squatting in front of her, looking up when he took her hands and curled them into his chest, his gaze so intense her stomach went haywire.

"I know what you're thinking," he said softly.

"Oh, really?"

"Mmm-hmm. That it's kind of hard to trust the future when the past hasn't exactly been your best friend. Believe me," he sighed out, "I know. I also know I gave up on you, on us, once before—"

"When we were seventeen? You're even counting that?"

"Actually, that was kind of my point. That while it's good to remember some parts of the past—the good parts— the crappy parts should probably be trashed." He touched her cheek. "And the woman I love now is so much more than the girl I thought I loved then. And I refuse to give up on that woman." A soft smile touched his lips. "I can't. Because you are the best damn thing to ever happen to me."

Tears filmed his eyes, making hers sting in response. "And if you say yes," he said thickly, "I will cherish you like nobody ever has before." One side of his mouth lifted. "And no secrets. Swearsies," he said, and a teary laugh bubbled from her chest.

Because there it was, the rock-solid steadiness she now realized she'd been missing, she'd been seeking, her entire adult life. Cole was so much like Pop, she thought with a start…despite her long-standing rebellion against the very thing she most needed. Wanted.

Deserved.

And damned if she was going to let fear stop her from having it.

Tearing up, she took his face in her hands. That dear, sweet face—the *right* face, she realized with a punch to the gut—that had meant so much to her all those years ago, that meant so much more to her now.

"Yes," she whispered, sure, and his smile warmed her

even more than the evening sunlight streaming through the grimy floor-to-ceiling windows, embracing them both.

Than the joy streaming through her, finally setting her free.

Epilogue

A year later

From the kitchen, while Kelly and assorted kids piled party food on platters, Cole spotted Bree out in the garden with her dad, the older man's arm slung around her shoulder. Cole knew how relieved she was that Preston had found his footing in his new digs, making friends and putting his two cents in about the landscaping whenever anyone would stop long enough to listen to him. Rumor had it that the old guy was dating again, too, although as of yet none of his kids had been able to get more than a "So what if I am?" out of him.

He also knew how relieved the Colonel was, in turn, that his oldest daughter was "settled," as he put it.

Behind him, family and friends celebrated his and Sabrina's low-key wedding with the usual raucous laughter and joking and very loud love that had always been part and parcel of any Noble gathering. His sister and her gang fit right in—and God knew Lizzie did—but he could tell his poor parents were a little overwhelmed by it all.

They'd get used to it, he thought, smiling.

The year hadn't been easy—he would never, ever, renovate an entire house from top to bottom again, especially one built during Teddy Roosevelt's administration—but the results were more than worth it. Sabrina had gotten the ball rolling, actually, enthusiastically overseeing the first stages of the remodel until Cole and the kids could finally join her in the city.

A city he was growing to love, surprisingly. As were his children, both thriving in their new school while reestablishing their relationship with Erin. Who'd apparently realized if she wanted to be a part of their lives, it was up to her to make that happen. Granted, nobody harbored any fantasies that she'd ever want to be a full-time mom again, but at least the visits were better.

And Bree had picked up the slack in that department like a champ. In fact, the other night he'd even heard her yell, "Because I said so!" up the stairs.

He was so proud of her he could pop.

And, yeah, he told her that. Every chance he got.

Both his wife and father-in-law turned as Cole swung open the French door, Bree's smile socking him right in the gut, as always. "I'll leave you two alone, then," Preston said, giving his daughter a quick kiss on her forehead before returning inside. But not before lightly punching Cole in his upper arm…and winking.

"Congratulations, Dad!"

Grinning, Cole took the older man's place to wrap his arms around Bree from behind and rest his chin in her curls. A light breeze whispered through the maple's thick leaves, a sweet top note to the gurgling fountain they'd put in earlier in the summer. Man, he loved this house.

His life.

This woman.

He slid one palm over her belly, slightly curved underneath her simple white dress. "So you told him?"

"I did. He's thrilled." Her soft laugh vibrated through him. "Almost as much as I am."

Her doctor had told her not to expect to get pregnant right away at her age. If she even would. Then again, she didn't know Sabrina Noble. Correction: Sabrina Noble Rayburn.

His meant-to-be wife.

The mother his children were meant to have.

He didn't have to ask her if she was happy, because he knew. Saw it, in her smile whenever she looked at him. Heard it, in her laughter when she was with the kids— who were every bit as excited about the baby as its parents.

"I love you, crazy woman," he murmured in her ear, making her shudder. And laugh.

"I love you, too," she whispered back, then turned in his arms to link her own around his neck, and he saw in her eyes a promise of forever.

A promise he captured with a kiss…as Wes yelled out the door, "Jeez, you guys—get a room!"

Chuckling, he met her sparkling gaze, brushing a wayward strand of hair off her temple. "A pair of teenagers *and* a newborn under the same roof? Are we insane?"

"Like you have to ask?" she said, then snuggled closer. And sighed.

And if he listened closely, he could hear the past whispering its blessings on their future…

* * * * *

MILLS & BOON®

The Sharon Kendrick Collection!

1 BOOK FREE!

Revenge is sweet

Eligible Bachelors

Society Secrets

Passion and seduction....

If you love a Greek tycoon, an Italian billionaire or a Spanish hero, then this collection is perfect for you. Get your hands on the six 3-in-1 romances from the outstanding Sharon Kendrick. Plus, with one book free, this offer is too good to miss!

Order yours today at
www.millsandboon.co.uk/Kendrickcollection

0415_ST_10

MILLS & BOON®

The Nora Roberts Collection!

1 BOOK FREE!

Don't miss this fantastic four-book collection from New York Times *bestselling author Nora Roberts.*

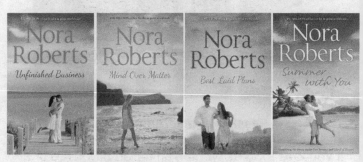

Don't miss this great offer—buy the collection today to get one book free!

Order yours at
www.millsandboon.co.uk/Noracollection

0415_ST_11

MILLS & BOON®

The Chatsfield Collection!

2 BOOKS FREE!

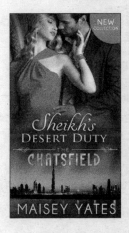

Style, spectacle, scandal…!

With the eight Chatsfield siblings happily married and settling down, it's time for a new generation of Chatsfields to shine, in this brand-new 8-book collection! The prospect of a merger with the Harrington family's boutique hotels will shape the future forever. But who will come out on top?

Find out at
www.millsandboon.co.uk/TheChatsfield2

CHATSFIELD_PROMO_BK

MILLS & BOON®

Cherish™

EXPERIENCE THE ULTIMATE RUSH OF FALLING IN LOVE

A sneak peek at next month's titles…

In stores from 17th April 2015:

- **The Pregnancy Secret** – Cara Colter
  and **Not Quite Married** – Christine Rimmer

- **A Bride for the Runaway Groom** – Scarlet Wilson
  and **My Fair Fortune** – Nancy Robards Thompson

In stores from 1st May 2015:

- **A Forever Kind of Family** – Brenda Harlen
  and **Bound by a Baby Bump** – Ellie Darkins

- **The Wedding Planner and the CEO** – Alison Roberts
  and **From Best Friend to Bride** – Jules Bennett

Available at WHSmith, Tesco, Asda, Eason, Amazon and Apple

Just can't wait?
Buy our books online a month before they hit the shops!
visit www.millsandboon.co.uk

These books are also available in eBook format!

Join our *EXCLUSIVE* eBook club

FROM JUST £1.99 A MONTH!

Never miss a book again with our hassle-free eBook subscription.

★ Pick how many titles you want from each series with our flexible subscription

★ Your titles are delivered to your device on the first of every month

★ Zero risk, zero obligation!

There really is nothing standing in the way of you and your favourite books!

Start your eBook subscription today at www.millsandboon.co.uk/subscribe

EBOOK_SUBS

"I'm almost afraid to ask what that was all about," Cole said, and she laughed.

"I'm almost afraid to tell you."

On a tight smile, Cole hitched up the knees of his khakis and lowered himself to the bench beside her. "But you're going to," he said, not looking at her. Unable to.

Sabrina laughed again, the sound as gentle as the early summer breeze dancing around them. "I was being grilled." When Cole's head swung to hers, she shrugged. "He was curious, understandably enough. About what we used to be to each other." She paused. "What we might be now. Especially since you apparently told him I saved your butt?"

Grimacing, Cole looked away again. "And what did you say?"

"That whatever we once were," she said softly, "it's in the past."

Her words should have been a relief. Which they were, in a way. Then why the sting? The stupid, totally illogical disappointment?

* * *

Jersey Boys:
Born...raised...and ready